An indecent proposal

"My nephew spoke to me about you," Brian Halloway said. "He wants you as his mistress."

The room tilted.

"I offered to find him a more suitable lover, but he's quite insistent he wants you."

Mistress? Lover? The words reverberated in her ears.

"Maids don't..."

"No, they don't. Not in this house. But I'm allowing you to become the exception. Are you attracted to my nephew, Justin?" Brian asked.

Maya's heart pummeled her chest. She wanted to lie, to say no, but she couldn't. "From the moment I first saw him." On the day he'd been kidnapped, she thought, wishing she hadn't gotten into this mess.

"Then you'll be with him?"

No, she thought. I can't sleep with a stranger, no matter how compelling he is.

"Yes. I'll be with him."

Dear Reader,

I'm thrilled to be part of the Silhouette Romantic Suspense line. I love this genre. What could be more exciting than writing a suspenseful story with love and desire leading the way?

Although this novel stands alone, it was born and bred from previous books—*Cherokee Baby, Cherokee Dad, Cherokee Stranger* and *A Kept Woman*. Over the years I've received letters about Justin Elk, who was ten months old in *Cherokee Dad,* my July 2003 Silhouette Desire Book. Readers wanted to see Justin all grown up, and they wondered if he would ever discover his mob roots.

I fast-forwarded in time, like the soap operas do with their kids, to write this book and make Justin a man. He is almost thirty now, and his life is about to take an unexpected turn. Not only does he discover who he is and where he came from, but also he falls for Maya Reyes, a beautiful young woman with family secrets of her own.

Thank you for your support and for picking up a copy of *Mob Mistress.* I hope it takes you on a journey that will entertain you to the very end.

Hugs,

Sheri WhiteFeather

Sheri WhiteFeather

MOB
MISTRESS

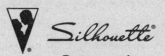

Romantic
SUSPENSE

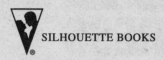

SILHOUETTE BOOKS

ISBN-13: 978-0-373-27539-7
ISBN-10:   0-373-27539-0

MOB MISTRESS

SHERI WHITEFEATHER

lives in a cowboy community in Central Valley, California. She loves being a writer and credits her husband, Dru, a tribally enrolled member of the Muscogee Creek Nation, for inspiring many of her American Indian–themed stories.

Sheri and Dru have two beautiful grown children and two pampered dogs, a border collie/Queensland heeler and a French bulldog. Sheri's hobbies include decorating with antiques and shopping in thrift stores for jackets from the 60s and 70s—items that mark her interest in vintage Western wear and hippie fringe.

To contact Sheri, learn more about her books and see pictures of her family, visit her Web Site at www.sheriwhitefeather.com.

To MJ for helping me write for the Romantic Suspense
line, to Patience for making me feel so welcome,
to Natashya for being my wonderful new editor,
and to Carl and Kim for the prison information.

Chapter 1

Justin Elk squinted in the darkness, his vision blurred, his temples throbbing. Blood pumped through his veins as thick and cumbersome as liquid lead.

The last thing he remembered was stopping at a roadside diner for a cup of coffee and a club sandwich. He'd been headed to the Gulf of Mexico, to loll on the beach, to enjoy a much-needed vacation.

And then he'd awakened here.

In an unfamiliar bed, stripped down to his jeans. His shirt and boots had been removed. His silver-buckled belt was gone, too.

He shifted his weight and cursed the emasculating wooziness. He'd been drugged. He could feel the sluggish beat of his heart, the sleep-induced, head-spinning intoxication.

Someone must have spiked his coffee at the diner. Slipped him a Mickey or whatever it was called. He'd gotten groggy when he'd climbed back into his truck, but at the time he wasn't sure why. He'd been too tired to drive, so he'd sat behind the wheel, trying to combat the sudden fatigue.

Which meant what? That they'd waited for him to conk out before they'd carted him off to…

He gripped the side of the massive bed, doing his damnedest to pull himself up.

His surroundings seemed grand, even in the vault of night. The sheets bunched beneath his fingers, the fabric soft and luxurious. Egyptian cotton, he thought. Probably four or five hundred bucks a pop. He'd never slept on anything this high-dollar before, but he knew how expensive quality linens could be. His family owned and operated a guest ranch that pampered its city-slicker guests.

He finally managed to sit upright and fumble for a lamp. With an unsteady grip, he illuminated the room.

The light glared straight at him, making pinwheels twist and turn before his eyes. Fighting another wave of dizziness, he turned his head, catching glimpses of his glamorous gilded cage.

Even though the furniture mutated in the drug-laced fog, he noticed opulent antiques. A French door, which he assumed was securely locked, showcased what appeared to be a terrace, and a hallway led to what he assumed was the rest of the suite. He suspected this was a guest room in someone's house.

Weren't kidnapping victims supposed to be bound and gagged and crammed into dark, dingy basements?

Whoever did this wasn't holding him for ransom. They probably had more money, more power, more social standing than his family could ever have.

He tried to drag himself out of bed, but before his feet hit the rippling floor, the whole damn room spun. Everything went by in a mindless blur.

Shit.

The sedative sluicing through his system was keeping him prisoner. He hoped that he didn't OD. He didn't want to croak in some rich man's castle. Then again, maybe the person who'd arranged his captivity was a woman.

Yeah, right. A decadent heiress just dying to have *him*, a Texas-bred horseman, as her sex slave. A Hill Country cowboy who gave riding lessons and guided tours.

Get real, he told himself. He hadn't been abducted because he looked good in a pair of Wranglers.

The room wouldn't quit spinning, so he turned off the lamp, shutting out the pinwheels, the glaring little lights flashing like camera bulbs beneath his eyes. He spewed a string of profanities and fought to stay conscious.

But he lost the battle and passed out again.

When Justin came to, he sensed the presence of another person.

Someone watching him.

Angry, he forced himself to sit up. He didn't care how wasted he was. This time he was going to pound his way out of this mess. But as he reached for the lamp to expose his captor, a woman's voice came out of the night.

"I unplugged it," she said. "I unplugged all of them."

Justin cursed. He couldn't very well pound a nameless, faceless female. Her tone was barely audible, barely above a whisper. He wondered if his heiress theory wasn't as far-fetched as it had seemed. "Who are you?"

"I can't tell you that. I'll get into trouble. I'm not supposed to be in your room."

Was this a game? Or was she on the level? He followed the direction of her voice and caught sight of her shadowy outline. She was only a few feet away.

Not that he could make out her features. He couldn't even distinguish the color or length of her hair. She seemed misty, like a ghost.

Or an angel.

Maybe he was dreaming. No, he thought. It was the drug. The room was spinning again.

"Are you okay?" she asked.

"That's a stupid question," he snapped. The digital clock on the nightstand displayed blurry red numbers. He had no idea what time it was, what day it was.

She moved closer, and he struggled to focus, to see her more clearly, but the runaway-carousel motion hadn't stopped.

When she touched him, placing a cool hand against his cheek, his heart bumped his chest.

"Is the medication making you nauseous?" she asked.

"Just dizzy." He tried to breathe in her scent, but she wasn't wearing a fragrance. Everything about her remained a mystery. "Are you a nurse?"

"No. But I saw them carry you in here, and I heard them talking about you. I could tell you were drugged." She removed her hand from his cheek, her featherlight touch fading. "I assume they've given you a couple of doses since then."

"How long have I been here?"

"Since yesterday. They said that you were important to them. That they're not going to hurt you."

"Who are *they*?" he asked, praying that she was being honest. That she wasn't part of the conspiracy.

"The West Coast Family," she responded.

"What?" Confused, he gazed at her hazy image.

"The media calls them the Hollywood Mob."

His befuddled brain kicked into gear. "The Halloways? That's who did this to me?"

"Yes." She sat on the edge of his bed, rustling the pricey sheets. "How well do you know them?"

"I don't know them at all. My uncle testified against Denny Halloway, their old boss, but that was ages ago. Twenty-nine years or so."

"Really?" She sounded surprised. "So that means Reed Blackwood is your uncle?"

"He's my mother's brother." Justin frowned, wondering why Reed's name came so easily to her. "He went into the witness protection program."

"Yes, I know. I read about him in old newspaper clippings."

He stalled, analyzing her response. If she were closely associated with the mob, she would have known about Reed firsthand.

"My uncle has never been part of my life," he said, admitting that he was scarcely related to the other man. "I was about a year old when he went into the program. He means nothing to me, and I mean nothing to him." He paused, curious about his surroundings. "Is this the Halloways' house?"

"Yes. You're in their mansion. In West L.A."

He contemplated what they'd done with his truck, if they'd hidden it somewhere. Surely they hadn't left it at the Texas diner where he'd been abducted.

"Do they have a private plane?" he asked.

"Yes."

"Do you think that's how they brought me here?"

"Probably."

When a sudden beat pulsed between them, he lifted his hand and attempted to touch her the way she'd touched him. For a split second, she seemed to sway closer to him. Then she pulled back, and he came up empty.

"Why did you sneak into my room? Why are you giving me information?"

"Because I want you to help me later."

He wanted to trust her. He wanted to believe that she was being sincere. But who the hell knew? "With what?" He squinted at her. Her hair was long and thick, he decided. Falling past her shoulders. Either that or the shifting shadows were playing tricks on his eyes.

"I can't tell you. Not now."

"Can you least tell me your first name?"

"No."

"Why not?"

"I need to be careful. I'm telling you things I'm not supposed to know." She stood up, leaving him alone on the bed. "There's something going on with a dead baby."

His blood drained from his face. He could feel the sudden clamminess of his skin.

Her voice went quieter, even more hushed. He had to lean forward to hear her.

"A baby's bones were discovered about a month ago. It was a newborn, buried in a makeshift coffin. Its death was never registered." She exhaled a fragile-sounding breath. "The Halloways think it's connected to you."

His stomach clenched. "I don't understand."

"Neither do I. But supposedly that baby has been dead for as long as you've been alive."

His mind reeled. "Who discovered it? And where was it found?"

"I don't know. But it was buried with a toy identical to one you had when you were little. A musical pony."

Justin went back to his childhood. He remembered his pony. His mom still had it somewhere. But she kept all sorts of sentimental stuff. "How do the Halloways know the toy was identical to mine?"

"I have no idea. I'm only repeating what I heard."

He made a face. An infant decomposing for thirty years was a ghastly image, especially with a stuffed pony that played a lullaby by its side. "Does Reed have anything to do with the baby? Did they mention him?"

"I didn't hear anyone say his name."

"Who was having this conversation?" he asked,

keeping his voice as low, as cautious as hers. "Exactly who did you eavesdrop on?"

"Denny Halloway's sons. Brian and his brother, Richard. They were talking to their security chief."

Justin pictured her skulking in a doorway, straining to hear their cryptic words. "Is Brian the boss?"

"Yes, and Richard is the underboss. But I only picked up bits and pieces of what they were saying."

"That they aren't going to hurt me? That I'm important to them?" His thoughts scattered. "Do you believe in ghosts?"

She hesitated, and he wondered if his question had given her goose bumps. He imagined her running her hands over her arms, up and down chilled skin.

"Do you?" she finally asked.

"Traditional Cherokees do," he responded.

"Are you Cherokee?"

"I'm a quarter-blood. From my father's side." He considered his culture. "They say that murdered souls are forced to roam the earth, unable to go to the next world."

"Why are you talking about murdered souls?"

"Because I think that baby was killed. Otherwise its death would have been registered. There would have been a legal burial."

"The Halloways didn't talk as if it had been murdered. It seemed important to them, too. Like you," she added softly.

"Me and a dead baby. How creepy is that?" He shook his head. "This is the strangest thing that's ever happened to me."

"It's strange for me, too. I keep hoping I'm doing the right thing. Involving you in my life."

Was that what she was doing? He couldn't tell. So far she'd revealed nothing about herself, nothing tangible, nothing he could grasp.

Moonlight drifted into the room, but it wasn't bright enough to illuminate her, to give him a clearer image.

Was she wearing a nightgown? Or a filmy dress? He noticed how flowing her garment looked, how sleek and watery.

Of course the Mickey medication was still messing with his mind, still distorting his vision.

But even so, he pictured her in silk. And he suspected that she was a brunette. Her hair seemed as dark as the night that shrouded them.

He fingered the sheet and felt it slide against his hand. "Are you as beautiful as I imagine you are?"

Her breath caught. He could hear the quick, sharp sound. "I didn't come here to feed your imagination, Justin."

"You know my name?"

"I heard them say it."

He knew it was crazy, but somewhere in his drugged-out mind, he was attracted to her, to a woman he couldn't even see. The whispered lilt of her voice sent God-help-me heat up his spine.

"Why didn't you call the police after you realized they'd kidnapped me?" he asked. "That's what most people would have done."

"I couldn't take that chance. If the Halloways found out it was me who made the call…"

"Dialing nine-one-one would've been easier than slipping into my room. You could have got police protection if you'd made the call."

"Yes, but I would have been forced to leave the mansion. And I want to stay here. I *need* to stay."

He couldn't begin to understand her. She talked in riddles. "Why?" he asked. "Tell me why you insist on living here. Give me a reason to help you."

She hesitated, and he waited.

Finally she gave in. Her voice turned sad, shaky, isolated. "Someone in my family went missing. I don't have any proof, but I believe the Halloways are involved." Silence fractured the air, then she added, "So will you promise to help me later? Will you promise to be there?"

He wasn't about to refuse. If the Halloways had kidnapped him, maybe they'd kidnapped her loved one, too? Then again, she kept saying the mob wasn't going to hurt him. "I promise. I'll do what I can." When he wasn't sedated, he thought. When he could think clearly.

"Thank you." She moved toward him. Within the blink of a blurry eye, she was almost touching him again.

Almost.

"I better go," she whispered. "But I'll try to come back tomorrow."

He kept silent. Next time he would make sure that he had access to a light so he could see her.

Next time?

He should be plotting an escape, but she compelled him instead, haunting him like the angel she was.

Her footsteps sounded softly. As she made her way to the door that would take her out of his suite and back to the mansion, he struggled to focus his gaze.

To watch her shadowy form disappear.

Sunshine blasted through the blinds, invading the room. Justin squinted at the clock. It was the middle of the afternoon.

He sat up and tested his equilibrium. He was hung over, feeling the aftereffects, but the drug it-self had worn off. Or so he hoped. He climbed out of bed and thanked the Creator when his feet hit solid ground.

And then his world went woozy again. Not liter-ally. But figuratively. A big clumsy puppy that had been sleeping on the floor jumped up and bounded toward him.

The black dog yipped and wiggled, but he could only stare. With its Dumbo ears and droopy eyes, the mutt looked like Chester, his childhood pet.

Only Chester had been dead for nineteen years.

"Where'd you come from?" he finally said.

The dog grinned in response. He wasn't Chester. He wasn't a canine ghost. But his uncanny resemblance to Justin's boyhood companion threw him for a loop.

Wary, he checked out the suite, the puppy on his heels. Nothing. No one. Nada. Whoever had dropped off the dog was gone.

So this time he took a closer look around. He went into the walk-in closet and saw that his suitcase had been unpacked. His clothes were hanging on wooden hangers. Even the shirt that had been stripped from him was there, laundered and pressed.

Apparently he was a welcome guest, a valued captive, just as his nighttime angel had said.

He walked into the bathroom. His toiletries, the travel-size toothbrush, toothpaste and shaving kit he'd brought along, were lined up on the counter. Complimentary bottles of shampoo, conditioner and liquid soap had been provided, much like a hotel. They were the brands he used at home.

He doubted the suite had been readied while he'd been occupying it. They'd probably done it before they'd even carried him in here.

The puppy pestered him for attention. He didn't want to get attached, so he ignored the goofy mutt and headed for the sitting room, where leather couches and an entertainment center dominated the masculine décor.

A sculpture by Frederic Remington, his favorite western artist, was displayed in a glass case. Justin had a recasting of it at home. But he suspected that this was the real deal.

Original Remingtons rarely came on the market, and when they did, major museums and private collectors scooped them up at astronomical prices.

But the Halloways could afford it, and he wouldn't be surprised if the statue had commanded a four or five-million-dollar price tag.

Had they purchased it to impress him? To entice him?

Taking a chance, he went to the main door and tried to open it. It didn't budge. It didn't even rattle. He was still holed up. But aside from the hangover, he was clearheaded, which meant the mob wanted him to be coherent. If they didn't, they would have sedated him again instead of dropping off a dog.

Justin checked the French door in the bedroom and discovered it was unlocked, the terrace providing a place for the pooch to pee. When he went outside, he realized that he was on the third floor.

He examined the view. Lush grounds erupted into

stone walkways, bubbling fountains and leafy plants and flowers.

Would this be his eventual escape route? Could he climb down the terrace without tripping an alarm? And if he got to the bottom safely, could he scale the cement wall that framed the yard and disappear without getting caught? Not likely. He spotted a uniformed guard at the edge of the building. But for now it didn't matter. He wasn't ready to leave, not until he found out why the mob had kidnapped him. And then, of course, there was his angel. Between his circumstances and hers, his mind was cluttered with unanswered questions. No, he thought. He wasn't about to attempt a premature escape.

Needing to combat his hangover, he took a shower. After soaping down and washing his hair, he combed it straight back and frowned at his hard-edged reflection in the mirror. His former fiancée used to say that he looked like a desperado, especially when he neglected to shave, so he grabbed a disposable razor and went to work on the stubble.

With a towel wrapped around his waist he came out of the bathroom, and the dog whined at him.

"Fine. I'll pet you." He reached down to scratch the mutt's elephant ears.

The happy-assed, ugly-as-sin dog rolled over on his back, exposing his belly and kicking his feet in the air.

So much for not getting attached. Justin decided to call him Lester since it rhymed with Chester.

He got dressed and took the puppy onto the terrace. Justin stood there for about fifteen minutes, checking out the situation again, wondering if he would be able to get past the guard at night, if when the time came, he could—

"I'd suggest using the stairs," a deep voice said from behind him.

He spun around and stared at the giant who'd uttered those smart-mouthed words.

Instinctively, Justin clenched his fists. His opponent outweighed him by at least eighty pounds, but Justin had the advantage of youth. The Hulk was probably on the far side of sixty.

"I'm glad you're up and about. But I figured you would be by now." The other man extended a beefy hand and introduced himself. "Leo Gordon. I'm in charge of security."

Justin didn't return the gesture. "Screw you," he said instead. He wanted to kick the crap out of the security chief, not make friends with him.

Leo grinned. He had a slightly crooked smile and a nose that had probably been broken a dozen times. His razor-buzzed, pseudo-military hair spiked into fuzzy gray points. He was dressed in a dark suit, as if he were trying to pass himself off as civilized. His shoes were high-dollar loafers.

"You've got balls," Leo said. "Like your old man."

Justin angled his head. "My old man?"

"Your dad. We were friends. Once upon a time."

Justin considered Michael Elk, his half-Cherokee father, the man who'd taught him right from wrong. Dad had been a hellion in his day, but his rebellious antics had been petty, smoking-in-the-boy's-room kind of stuff, not consorting with the mob. That had been Uncle Reed's turf. Or so Justin had been told. But now he didn't know what to think.

Unfazed by the tension, Lester yapped happily at Leo, and the security chief picked him up, allowing the mutt to give him an affectionate nuzzle. But he'd probably brought the puppy to the room to begin with.

"Where am I?" Justin asked, pretending that he wasn't aware of his surroundings. That he didn't have an angel on his side. "Whose house is this?"

"It's the Halloway mansion." Leo cradled the dog.

"Halloway?" He repeated the name, playing his part, doing his damnedest to seem surprised. "Like the Hollywood Mob?"

"You catch on quick, kid." Leo didn't smile. No more half-cocked expressions. "We need to cut the chitchat and get going. Your family is anxious to see you."

Justin flinched. His parents were here? Had they been abducted, too? And what about his sister? She was in Europe, but had they gotten to her, as well? "My family? If you did anything to them, I'll kill you."

"Lighten up. They're fine. Now let's go."

Justin followed Leo out of the suite and into the mansion, where the architecture made an affluent statement. When they came to a sweeping staircase, Leo started his descent. Lester rode with his chin propped on the security chief's shoulder.

The puppy gazed at Justin and barked excitedly, as if they were on a grand adventure. Leo didn't falter. He simply patted the dog to quiet him.

When they reached a black-and-white tiled foyer, the other man finally stopped and turned. "This way," he said, indicating a gentleman's parlor.

Sturdy sofas and wing-back chairs governed the room, with chestnut tables and built-in bookcases.

Justin glanced around, looking for familiar faces. But the parlor was empty. "Where's my family?"

"They'll be here." Leo put Lester down, and the puppy scampered around. "Why don't you have a seat?"

"I prefer to stand."

"Suit yourself." Leo stood, too. He took an unassuming spot by a window where burgundy drapes, loaded with tassels and trim, were open, displaying a cluster of palm trees and a rolling-green lawn. As he adjusted his jacket, he flashed the holstered gun clipped to his belt.

Justin gave him a hard look. He wanted to jam his fist down the security chief's throat. And he would, when all of this was over, when he knew his family was safe.

A uniformed maid wheeled a serving cart into the office, and Leo snapped at her. "You're intruding on a private meeting."

"I'm sorry, sir," she responded in a respectful tone. "But the chef sent me. Mr. B. requested some hors d'oeuvres."

Leo waved his hand, allowing her to proceed.

Justin assumed that Mr. B. was Brian Halloway, the boss. Referring to him as Mr. Halloway was probably confusing since there was more than one Mr. Halloway at the mansion. The angel had mentioned Richard Halloway, too.

The dog, curled up in the corner, perked his ears as the maid pushed the cart farther into the room.

Justin took a closer look at her, and when he did, his pulse jammed his throat.

Her hair, dark and rich, was coiled into a tidy bun, exposing the stunning angles of her face. Her bronze-toned skin appeared soft and touchable, and the greenish-gold color of her eyes enhanced what Justin called ethnic ambiguity. He had a similar look. People were never quite sure of his heritage.

She was what he imagined his angel to be. Sleek, sexy, exotic. But she was cautious and proper, too.

She moved around the room without disturbing him.

He wanted to catch her gaze, to force her to look at him, but she focused on her task, arranging the appetizers just so.

Was she the mystery lady who'd come to his room? Or was he grasping at straws? Wrongly evaluating the first woman he saw? Maybe if he heard her speak again. Maybe her voice…

"What's your name?" he asked her.

She took an audible breath, and Leo frowned.

"If you're itching for female companionship, we can get you a woman," the security chief told Justin, not allowing the maid to answer.

Damn it. Justin cursed his mistake. He hadn't meant to be so obvious, so openly attracted to her. "I'm not itching for anything, I just want to know her name."

Leo gestured for her to respond.

"It's Maya," she said, keeping her eyes downcast and fussing with a silver coffee service. "Maya Reyes."

Her voice didn't trigger familiarity. But he couldn't ask her to whisper, to talk in a softer tone, to mimic his angel. "That's a pretty name."

"Thank you." She finished her work and left the parlor without meeting his gaze.

"She's supposed to know her place," Leo said. "All of our employees are."

Irritated, Justin glared at the Hulk. "What's taking this meeting so long to happen?"

Leo shrugged.

But several minutes later he announced that Brian Halloway had just entered the room. Tall and trim with graying blond hair, Brian carried himself like a corporate billionaire, exhibiting a commanding sense of style.

He extended his hand, but Justin refused to shake it, spurning him the way he'd spurned Leo.

"What's wrong?" Brian asked, a humorous glint in his eye. "Were you expecting Tony Soprano?"

Justin remained silent. He knew the West Coast Family wasn't an Italian outfit. They were equal-opportunity criminals.

"My brother asked me to apologize for his absence. Richard intended to be here, but he got called away on a business trip." Brian remained standing. "He's looking forward to meeting you."

Justin snapped back. "I don't care about your brother. And I don't give a damn about you. I want to see my parents. And my sister, if she's here."

Brian made a perplexed expression. "I don't understand."

"Your security chief said my family was anxious to see me."

"Your family, yes. Your parents and sister, no. Leo misled you." Brian frowned at the Hulk, but the big man kept his cool. He didn't even blink.

The boss returned his attention to Justin, playing

the ultimate host. "Can I get you something? Crab canapés? Garlic and cheese bruschetta? Liver paté? You must be starving by now. This should hold you over until dinner."

Screw the food. Justin didn't care if he hadn't eaten in two days. "I want to know what the hell is going on."

"Then I'll tell you, straight from the hip. I'm your family. Me, my brother." The mobster held his gaze. "You're not Justin Elk." He paused for effect. "You're Justin Halloway."

Chapter 2

Justin glared at the other man. "What kind of game are you playing?"

"No game. Your mother was my sister, Beverly. She died without telling us that she'd had a child."

His gut tightened, tying itself into ropey knots. "This has to be a mistake."

"It's the truth. I've got the DNA test to prove it. We swabbed you while you were sedated." Brian reached into his jacket pocket and removed a sealed envelope. "You're welcome to review the results."

Justin took the envelope, but he didn't open it. He

wouldn't give Brian the satisfaction. "If Beverly's my mother, then who's my father?"

The boss made a distasteful face. "Reed Blackwood."

The man he'd been told was his uncle? He glanced at Leo. Reed was the once-upon-a-time friend the security chief had mentioned. "My parents wouldn't have lied to me. They wouldn't have let me think that I was their son."

"But they did, Justin. Look at the report."

"This could be a forgery."

"You're right. It could be, but it isn't." The mobster poured a cup of coffee and took a sip. "Being a Halloway is your legacy, your birthright. Whether you like it or not."

"You drugged me. You kidnapped me." Justin all but snarled. "What kind of legacy, what kind of birthright is that?"

"We got your attention, didn't we? And no matter how much you try to deny it, we added some excitement to your life." Brian had the gall to smile. "We know you were restless. That your daily routine was getting mundane. Besides, if the test had been negative, we would have returned you to Texas and never revealed ourselves." He glanced at Lester, and the pooch wagged his tail. "We would have sent the dog along, too." He smiled again. "And the Remington."

Justin squinted. They would have given him a
four-to-five-million-dollar statue for the inconve-
nience? Talk about having money to burn. "That
sounds like a better deal to me."

"What does? Not being related to us and going
home with a costly consolation prize? Your inheri-
tance is worth far more than that, nephew. And the
Remington is yours either way."

Nephew? "No harm? No foul?"

"Exactly."

Except for his angel, Justin thought. The woman
who'd already told him who they were. "I could press
charges against you."

Brian tilted his head. "Yes, you could. Kidnapping
is a federal offense."

How poised could the other man be? How calm?
How sure of himself? "But you don't think I will, do
you?"

"No. I think you need us. That there's an empti-
ness inside of you we can fill. And we need you,
too. You're all that's left of Beverly. I can't tell you
how much we loved your mother. How special she
was to us."

Justin bent the corner of the envelope. He still
hadn't opened it, still hadn't looked at the results. He
nailed Brian's gaze instead. "My mother's name is
Heather Elk."

"Heather raised you, but she isn't your biological

mother." Brian tasted the pate. "Do you know how we figured out that you might be Beverly's son? My father, your grandfather, came across a newspaper article in the prison library about a dead baby, and it triggered his memory. Something from the past."

Justin turned morbidly silent, as though he hadn't heard about the infant before now.

Brian continued, "The police were looking for the public's help to identify the baby. They offered all sorts of details. They said it was a newborn that had been dead for thirty years. A boy with Native American genetics. They can tell a lot about a corpse by its bones." He finished the appetizer. "Dad knew he'd stumbled onto something. The location where they'd found the baby rang a bell. Thirty years ago, we tracked Reed, Beverly and Heather there."

"Why?"

"To kill Reed and bring Beverly home. They'd run off to elope, and Heather was trying to help them. They all managed to escape. This was before Reed went into WITSEC. Witness Security," Brian clarified.

"That still doesn't explain my paternity."

"Both women were pregnant. Of course at the time we didn't know there was one baby, let alone two. Reed, Beverly and Heather were on the run for eighteen months. Even Michael had no idea where they were. When Heather and Beverly returned on their own, Beverly was terminally ill, and Heather presented Michael with a ten-month-old son."

"Me?"

"Yes, you. As far as we can figure, their real child died and was secretly buried. It's the infant that was found, the one Dad read about. According to the article, it was laid to rest with a toy, a windup pony. And guess what? We discovered that you had one just like it. We got a hold of old photographs. You used to cart that thing everywhere."

Justin narrowed his gaze. It was obvious they'd been investigating every aspect of his life, past and present, making sure he was connected to the dead baby before they kidnapped him. "So Beverly came home to die, Reed struck a deal with the government, and Heather and Michael became my parents?"

"Only it was Beverly who conceived you with that traitor lover of hers." A slight pause. A slight thought. "Did you know that Reed was a West Coast Family soldier? Besides being an ex-con and an accomplished thief, he had a genius IQ and built countersurvelliance equipment in his spare time. He impressed us at first, especially Dad."

"What does that have to do with me?"

"We're aware that you have a genius IQ, too."

Meaning what? That he'd inherited his superior intelligence from a guy with no morals?

Justin finally opened the sealed envelope and

looked at the contents. 99.9 percent positive. He wanted to crumble it, to trash it, but that wouldn't change the results. He steeled his emotions instead.

The other man waited a beat, then continued, "When Reed seduced Beverly, all hell broke loose. She was a college student, the pride of our daddy's eye. In the old mob way, you're supposed to ask for permission to date the boss's daughter."

"So why didn't Reed ask?"

"Because he botched up a job he was sent to do, and Dad stopped trusting him. There was no way he was going to let him keep seeing Beverly. He warned Reed to stay away from his daughter."

"So Reed convinced Beverly to run away with him?"

"Exactly. And then Heather got dragged into it. She was naïve when it came to her brother."

Justin gripped the back of a wing back chair. His mother rarely talked about Reed. Aside from admitting that he'd testified against Denny Halloway and entered the witness protection program, she kept her memories to herself.

"That bastard left you behind," Brian said. "He could have taken you into WITSEC with him, but he couldn't be bothered. You'd do well to hate him."

"Don't tell me how to feel," Justin shot back, even though he *was* starting to despise Reed. "What's the deal with Beverly? Why didn't she admit to her family that I was her son? Why the big charade?"

"Beverly loved us, but she detested our lifestyle. I guess she thought you'd be better off without us."

"I can't say I blame her."

"We're different now."

Justin blinked. "What?"

"We're not involved in organized crime anymore. People still associate us with it, of course. But all of our businesses are legitimate now."

Yeah, right. He might have been born under shaky circumstances, but he hadn't been born yesterday. "You actually expect me to believe that?"

Brian laughed a little. "No, I suppose not. Not after we kidnapped you. But aside from that, we haven't broken the law in years. Richard and I weeded out the bad blood in our organization. We made a conscious choice to change who and what we are."

Justin glanced at Leo, but the security chief didn't react. He stood like a sentry, gun clipped to his belt, with the sun illuminating his Hulkish form.

People don't change, he thought. Not like that. "Whose idea was it to kidnap me?"

"Dad's."

"So he's still calling the shots? Even though he's locked up?"

"Dad thought it was important to expose you to the kind of power our family wields. Whether we're criminals or not."

"I don't give a crap about your power."

"Eventually you will. Once you get past the kidnapping, you'll enjoy the entitlement that comes with being a Halloway. And you'll admit that your life was getting boring. That we managed to spice it up."

Screw this. "I'm going back to Texas."

"What for?"

"Why the hell do you think? To talk to my mom and dad." To rage, to vent, he thought. To fight the pain, the lies, the deceit.

"We were hoping that you'd spend the rest of your vacation with us." Brian made a joke. "After all the trouble it took to get you here."

Frustration hit him hard and quick. He wasn't in the mood for petty humor.

The other man caught his scowl and turned serious. "Are you angry at your parents?"

Justin didn't answer the question. He spun it around on his supposedly "reformed" mobster uncle. "Are you mad at Beverly for keeping the truth from you?"

"It's tough to be angry at someone who's gone, who died so tragically. But I wish she had allowed us the opportunity to know you when you were young. That she wouldn't have robbed us of her son."

"It could have turned out the other way. The other baby could have been Beverly and Reed's child."

"Yes, it could have. And we would have notified the authorities if that had been the case. We would have asked for its remains so we could give it a decent burial. I imagine Heather and Michael will want to do that. But the police will probably grill them. They'll have to answer some difficult questions. According to the article we read, this is being treated like a homicide."

Justin nodded. He'd assumed the infant had been murdered, too.

"After you go home, after you settle things in Texas, will you come back?" Brian asked. "Will you visit with us? Will you give us a chance?"

Justin stalled, thinking about his angel, about the possibility that she was Maya, the maid who'd been too uncomfortable to meet his gaze. How could he keep his promise to her if he didn't return?

"We'd like to make a formal announcement," Brian added. "Introduce you to the rest of the family and tell all of our friends who you are. Maybe host a few parties."

Parties? Justin snagged Leo's gaze and felt his bones go cold. He didn't want to get caught up in being the long-lost nephew, in being Denny Halloway's revered grandson, in having men like Leo standing guard. But he'd already made his mind up earlier that he wasn't going to abandon the woman who'd asked for his help.

"Our pilot can take you to Texas," Brian said. "And he can bring you back. It's the family jet. That's what it's for."

"Where's my truck?"

"Here. In the garage. But you're not going to drive, are you?"

"No. I'll fly. On your jet," Justin responded, praying that he was making the right choice.

That his angel was worth it.

The chef scowled at Maya. A wiry man with a shaved head and a neatly trimmed goatee, he used his apron strings like tentacles.

Maya didn't like him. But none of the kitchen maids did. Behind his back, they called him Lucifer.

She finished preparing the cart, and he peered over her shoulder, inspecting her work.

Several hours after Justin had attended the private meeting, he'd ordered dinner for himself and the puppy she'd seen in the parlor. Or she assumed it was Justin who'd requested the meal. He was the only visitor at the mansion.

"Maids aren't allowed to consort with guests," Lucifer said, lifting his pointy nose at her.

Her pulse wouldn't quit pounding. "I know."

"Mr. Elk specifically asked for you."

Damn, she thought. *Damn.* "I didn't provoke that." Nor had she known that Justin's last name was Elk.

The chef measured her. "I certainly hope not. Now get going. He's in the Garden Tower."

Maya didn't respond. The suite where Justin had

been held hostage, the room she'd secretly visited, was aptly named, towering over the garden with a prestigious view.

She took the service elevator to the third floor and traveled down what suddenly seemed like an endless hallway.

She knocked on Justin's door, and he gave her permission to enter.

Maya wheeled the cart into the sitting room, and the puppy ran toward her. Justin stood beside the sofa. Tall and dark with rangy muscles, he shifted his stance. His hair rebelled against the way he wore it, falling onto his forehead even though he'd combed it straight back. A glimmer of silver winked in his left ear. She hadn't noticed the tiny hoop before, but it fit his Cherokee side, the quarter-blood roots he'd told her about.

Taking a deep breath, she warned herself to relax. When she looked up and met his gaze, she saw the scrutiny in his eyes.

He suspected her.

"Where would you like to eat?" she asked.

He kept watching her, trying to figure her out. "At the table is fine."

She moved toward the cozy dining area. Sniffing the air, the puppy followed.

"You can put his bowl on the floor," Justin said.

She nodded and gave the dog his food. He ate it noisily, wolfing it down with chowhound vigor.

As she arranged Justin's silverware, her heart struck her chest. He hadn't taken his eyes off of her, not even to blink.

She struggled to keep her distance, to not give herself away. Or to admit that she was attracted to him. That sitting beside him on his bed and brushing her hand along his cheek had made her warm.

Erotically warm.

"Do you know why I'm here?" he asked, attempting to call her bluff.

She didn't respond.

"Because I'm a Halloway," he told her. "A long-lost relative."

Maya dropped his salad fork, and it chimed against the table. She recovered it quickly, but the damage was already done. Justin gauged her reaction, watching her with keener interest.

She'd sneaked into his room because she needed an ally. Because she was hoping that a man who'd been kidnapped would jump at the chance to fight back. But if she'd known who he was, she would've *never* approached him.

"According to Brian, my mother was his sister." He pushed his hair back, battling the rain-straight rebellion. "Her name was Beverly. She's dead now."

Maya tried to focus on her job, to pour his wine, but her hand wouldn't quit shaking. She'd seen Beverly's portrait in the den, hanging on the wall like a shrine.

No wonder Justin was important to the Halloways. No wonder they hadn't intended to hurt him.

How stupid could she be, seeking him out? But worse yet was admitting that someone in her family had gone missing. What if he told the Halloways? What if they found a way to connect her to her dad?

Justin pulled up a chair and sat at the table, forcing his proximity, making Maya lose her train of thought. Her mind was twirling like a press-and-spin top. She struggled to serve his meal.

"They said that Reed Blackwood is my father. But I always thought he was my uncle."

She tried not to flinch. He was bringing up Reed's name to get her reaction. She'd already told him that she'd read about his uncle…his dad. Heaven help her.

"I'm returning to Texas in the morning," Justin said. "That's where I'm from. I wasn't sure if you were aware of that."

"Then I hope you have a good trip," she finally responded, trying to sound like a proper maid, as if she didn't know anything about him.

"I'm coming back. I made a special promise to someone."

She swallowed the lump in her throat. He was staring straight at her, holding her captive. Kidnapping her the way the mob had kidnapped him.

"You don't talk much, do you?" he asked.

She glanced away. "I'm not supposed to get too friendly with guests."

"There's no one here but us."

"You requested me by name. You shouldn't have done that." Beyond nervous, she placed his dessert on the table. "You'll get me fired."

"No, I won't. I'm a Halloway, remember?" He made a grand gesture. "One of the lords of the manor."

"I'm not supposed to get overly familiar with family members, either."

"I'm not telling you anything that you won't find out about later." He reached for his wine. "Brian wants to make a formal announcement. To introduce me to the rest of the Halloways. To host a few parties in my honor." He paused, tasted the chardonnay. "Not that there won't be a few skeletons left over in my closet."

Like the dead baby? He hadn't mentioned that. But it must have something to with his paternity.

"If there isn't anything else I can get you, then I should go. The chef—"

"Warned you not to get too familiar with me?" He kept watching her.

"Yes." She couldn't think clearly, not with him looking at her like that.

"I'm not trying to get you into trouble, Maya."

No, she thought. He was waiting for her to come clean, to tell him who she was. But she couldn't bring herself to do it, and he didn't ask her directly, just in case she was the wrong girl.

"Will you look after Lester while I'm gone?" he asked instead.

She frowned. "Lester?"

He pointed to the dog, and the puppy danced in a circle. "He was a gift from the Halloways. He looks a lot like my childhood pet. It was tough to resist him."

She glanced at the mixed-breed. He was so ugly he was cute. "I shouldn't—"

"Get overly familiar with my dog? What's the harm in that?"

She wanted to trust Justin. She wanted to believe that he was as honest as he seemed. "No harm," she said, taking a small chance.

He smiled, revealing a set of boyishly lethal dimples, making her wonder what she'd gotten herself into. He actually turned her knees weak. How sexy could he be?

"I'll tell Brian I'm leaving Lester in your care." The dimples faded. He was no longer smiling. "It's going to be tough seeing my parents. I'll be glad to get it over with."

She tried to seem unaffected, but she couldn't help thinking about her own parents and the secret they'd kept.

"Are you okay?" he asked, as a shiver sliced her spine.

She looked up at the man who'd promised to help her. A man whose new family she believed was responsible for whatever had happened to her dad. "I'm fine." She glanced at the food he'd yet to eat. "Just put the dishes outside of your door when you're done."

He reached out to brush her arm. "Are you sure you're all right?"

"Yes." His concern, his deliberate touch, made her weak-kneed all over again.

A moment later, she left his room, anxious for him to return to the mansion.

And wishing to God she wasn't.

Chapter 3

Justin sat on his parents' porch. The red-and-white farmhouse was as familiar as the beat of his heart. Bluebonnets bloomed every spring, and a live oak in the front yard clawed its way to the sky.

But it gave him no peace.

He'd grown up at Elk Ridge Ranch: the five-star guest lodge, the rustic rental cabins, the grassy slopes, the limestone caves. His own house, a log dwelling in the hills, was his sanctuary.

Or so he'd thought. Today he felt disconnected from everything, even the loving, caring people who'd raised him.

He turned to look at his dad. At fifty-five Michael Elk was strong and well built. Although his hair was streaked with gray and had thinned a bit over the years, he still wore it long and banded into a ponytail, the way a lot of older Indians did.

Justin had expected to age just like him, to get sun-burnished lines at the corners of his eyes, to see a recognizable image in the mirror. But how was that possible? They weren't related, not by blood.

He studied his mom next. Heather Elk. He remembered when she was pregnant with his sister. He'd touched her tummy and asked her if he'd lived inside of her, too. And she'd scooped him up and told him that he had. He'd cuddled in her arms, thinking she was the most beautiful mommy on earth, with her princess-in-the-tower hair and crayon-blue eyes.

"I'm sorry," she said, her voice breaking.

"For what? Lying to me?" Justin was supposed to be part white because of her. But it was Beverly who'd given him his Anglo roots. And Reed who made him part Indian. His mom's half brother was half-Cherokee. "How'd you fake my birth certificate?"

A strand of white-blond hair fluttered across her cheek. "It's a legitimate document, but it was filed ten months after you were born."

With phony information, he thought. "When I was a kid, you told me that the photo album with my early baby pictures had been lost. But that was a lie, too. There are no pictures. You couldn't snap them while you were on the run."

"No, we couldn't," she responded simply.

He pressed her, wanting answers, wanting to know about the other child. "Did your real son have a name? Did you give him one before you buried him?"

"You are our real son, Justin. We love you more than any parent could love a child." She shifted in her chair, fought the tears in her eyes. "But no, I didn't name him. Reed said we should name our children the Cherokee way, to wait until we saw them, until they were born. Reed delivered both babies. We couldn't go to a hospital. We couldn't take that chance." She paused, still fighting tears. "You were born first. About a week later, I went into labor, but the child in my womb was stillborn. The umbilical cord got…"

Her words faded, and Justin glanced up at the sky. Soon the sun would be setting, melding into the clouds, getting darker, preparing for the coffinlike closure of night. He wanted to console his mom, to ease her pain, but his own hurt and anger blocked the way.

"I took you and your dad to the place he was buried," she said suddenly. "After Reed went into WITSEC, after Beverly died. I took both of you there."

He tried to envision the unmarked grave, but being switched with a dead baby only gave him a chill. "Why?"

"Because I needed to see where he was laid to

rest," his dad interjected. "And we wanted to tell you about him. You were too young to understand, only about a year old, but it mattered to us."

"We told you that he had a pony just like yours," Mom added. "That mattered, too."

"The toy that Denny Halloway read about," Justin said.

Dad made a tight face. "Denny was a snake. I'm sure he still is."

"Yeah, but you should have told me the truth. Not when I was a baby, but when I was old enough to understand. I should have been given some sort of choice."

"To do what? Meet Beverly's family?" His mom exhaled a shaky breath. "They would have fought for custody. And with their power and law-bending privilege, they probably would have bribed a corrupt judge and won."

"They got me now, didn't they? They came into my life just the same."

"By kidnapping you?" Dad's voice turned hard. "I could kill them for that."

"They didn't hurt me." He wasn't sure why he was making excuses for his abductors. All he knew was that his world had been turned inside out and that his parents' lie had triggered it.

Mom's eyes filled up again. "I promised Beverly and Reed that I would keep their secret. They loved you. And they loved each other. They would have raised you if they could."

Justin scowled, repeating what Brian had said. "Reed could've taken me into WITSEC with him. He didn't have to give me up."

"The FBI didn't offer Reed a deal until after I brought Beverly home to die, until after she told the Halloways that you were mine. How would we have explained my son going into witness protection with my brother? The Halloways would have figured out the truth."

"Couldn't the government have faked my death or something? Then whisked me off to be with Reed?"

"I suppose they could have. But Reed never told the government that you were his son. He wanted you to stay with us. To have a normal childhood."

No, Justin thought. Reed was trying to make things easier for himself. "Have you heard from him since he went into witness protection? Is he allowed to keep in touch?"

"WITSEC permits government-screened phone calls and letters, but Reed asked his field inspector to contact us instead. About a year after he testified against Denny, we were told that Reed was doing well. That he met a nice girl and got married."

Well, bully for him. "Does he have other kids?"

"I don't know. We only heard from his inspector that one time. I think Reed needed to sever those ties, to convince himself that he was doing the right thing. I can't tell you how many times he cried about letting you go."

Yeah, right. The grieving father. "Brian says you're naive, Mom. That you trusted Reed too much."

"Brian? You mean Denny's son? They had a hit out on my brother. They still do. If they didn't, Reed would be able to come home."

"After all this time? What's the point? He has a new name, a new life. He isn't your brother anymore."

"He'll always be family. *Always,*" she reiterated.

Not to me, Justin thought.

"Don't go back to California," his mom implored, as if she'd read his mind. "Please. Don't go back."

"I have to."

"For the girl who came to your room?"

He nodded. He'd told his parents about his angel, but he hadn't told them that he suspected a maid. That the more he thought about it, the more he knew she was the one. She'd reacted too strongly to him being a Halloway. She'd given herself away, and the next time he saw her, he was going to press her even further.

"Why can't you call the police?" his mom asked. "Why can't you let them help her?"

"She doesn't want to call the cops. She suspects the Halloways of something, but she doesn't have any proof."

Mom refused to back down. "Anything that involves them is dangerous. You know it is."

Yes, he knew, but he responded with a stupid comment. "Brian says the Hollywood Mob doesn't exist anymore."

Both of his parents gave him an incredulous look.

"Other crime families have disbanded. So why not them?" He defended the Halloways, and this time he knew why. He didn't want to admit that his genes were so horribly tainted. That the mobsters who wanted to embrace him so badly were making Maya afraid.

His dad scooted forward. "Don't fall into their trap. Don't let them lure you into all that phony glamour. Don't do what Reed did."

"I'm not like Reed," Justin snapped, resenting the comparison.

"Then help the girl who needs you and come home."

Home? At this point, he didn't even know what the word meant. But worse yet was his dilemma with Maya.

And how he was going to help her without getting caught.

Justin was back. Maya hadn't seen him, but she'd heard that he'd returned last night.

The mansion buzzed with activity. Today the staff was preparing for a poolside gathering. A family-and-close-friends event: casual food and games for the children, sushi, sashimi and sake for the adults.

Maya still had Justin's puppy. He followed her around the state-of-the-art, chrome-and-glass kitchen, sniffing for tidbits. Lucifer hadn't uttered a word. But what could the chef say? Lester was Justin's pet, and Justin was the Halloway golden boy. By now, everyone in the house had been informed that he was Beverly's secret son.

And this was his coming-out party, Maya thought, his first soiree with his new family.

Suddenly Brian's girlfriend swept into the room. Dressed for the festivities in a designer swimsuit and a matching cover-up, she flaunted her outfit. Her sandals sparkled with glass beads and gold braid.

Like Lucifer, she'd been christened behind her back. Her name was Tori Temple, but the maids called her Tori Tell All because she talked out of turn, telling them things she shouldn't. She wasn't the brightest bulb in the chandelier, but she had legs like a Victoria's Secret model and hair like Lady Godiva.

She'd been one of many mistresses who'd broken up Brian's marriage. His wife had gotten tired of his philandering ways and had filed for divorce, taking a hefty chunk of change with her.

But before the ink on the financial settlement had dried, Tori Tell All had maneuvered her way into the mansion, traipsing around like the blow-up doll she was.

Not that Brian was faithful to her. According to rumor, he still kept his other bimbos on the side. The Halloway men didn't know the meaning of commitment.

Tori snagged a seafood-stuffed norimaki off a platter and bit into it. Lucifer's expression didn't falter, but he was probably cringing inside. Rice trickled onto the floor, breaking free of the seaweed wrap.

The leggy blonde finished the sushi roll. "I just love these." She looked at Maya. "Don't you?"

"They're the chef's specialty," Maya responded, as the puppy in her care lapped up the loose rice.

Tori reached down to pat his head, exposing her cosmetically enhanced cleavage. "Brian told me to invite some girls for Justin. You know, so he could take his pick."

Something akin to jealousy reared its ugly head, but Maya didn't react, not visibly.

Brian's mistress kept blabbing. "A blonde, a brunette and a redhead." She went after another norimaki. "We aren't sure what type he likes best."

Another maid shot Maya a "be careful" look. Whenever Tell All talked too much, *they* got in trouble for gossiping, even if they hadn't said a thing.

"I hope this doesn't make me seem like Heidi Fleiss." Tori made a face. "They're starlets, not hookers." She finished the sushi, dropping more rice for the puppy to lap up. "I met Justin this morning. He's handsome, don't you think? Dark and sexy."

Maya wasn't about to respond.

"Oh!" The blonde yipped. "Speak of the Texan. There he is."

Yes, there he was, entering the kitchen. But as dark and sexy as he was, he didn't look like a Texan today. Like Tori, he was dressed for the party. He wore surfer-style swim trunks.

Maya tried not to notice his body: his chest, his stomach, the athletic way in which he moved.

He walked up to her. "I'm here to collect my dog."

She merely nodded. Tori watched them with blatant interest.

"Was he good?" Justin asked.

"Yes, he—" Maya stammered.

"He what?"

"Nothing," she said. Lester had slept in her bed, curling into a furry ball, keeping her warm at night.

"Will you get him for me?"

"Yes, of course." The dog wasn't paying them any mind. He was too busy sniffing the floor, scouting morsels he might have missed.

She reached for Lester, wondering what Justin was up to. He could have managed the dog far better than she could. The big, overgrown puppy was a cumbersome bundle.

Was Justin playing his lord of the manor role? Making a maid do his bidding? Or was—

Maya froze. He moved in close, *too* close, to transfer the dog into his arms. When he brushed his lips against her ear, she went woozy.

"Tell me you're *her*," he whispered, keeping his words so soft, so low, even Maya barely heard. "Tell me."

Dear God.

She could see the just-do-it frustration in his eyes. But she saw something else, too. Heat. Hunger. The peril of desire.

Struggling for composure, she backed away from him, from the heart-palpitating intimacy. For what seemed like a long, drawn-out moment, their gazes locked.

No one said anything. A pin could have dropped. Finally he shifted the squirming puppy, and she glanced away.

"You like brunettes," Tori blurted.

Justin blinked, turned, addressed her. "What?"

"They're your favorite."

"That's right, they are," he admitted, looking directly at Maya before he left the kitchen.

She went to the sink to wash her trembling hands, and Lucifer raised his demonic eyebrows at her, scolding her in silence. If he only knew.

Tori ignored them and flitted out of the room. To

invite more brunettes to the party, Maya thought. To amuse Justin. To give him a smorgasbord of what he liked best.

Women who resembled the dark-haired maid.

The backyard offered an Olympic size pool, a rain forest waterfall, a barbecue island and an oasis of palm trees.

Justin sat on a chaise lounge with a plate of Japanese delicacies and a cup of sake by his side.

The experience was surreal. Kids, ranging from toddlers to teens, played in the sun, and gorgeous girls in eye-popping bikinis showed off their tans.

The bevy of brunettes, he'd learned, was for him.

Not that he was interested. He kept looking for Maya, watching the buffet table, waiting for her to replenish it.

A shadow crossed in front of him. "Are you having a good time?"

He squinted at the sun-hazed figure and realized it was Richard Halloway, his other uncle. He'd met Richard briefly last night when the other man had returned from his business trip.

Richard didn't seem like a mobster. He wasn't trim and tailored like Brian nor was he tough and terse like Leo. With his thinning brown hair, wire-framed glasses and slight paunch, he came off as a regular fifty-something guy.

He sat beside Justin and put his drink on a tiki-style table. "So are you?"

"Enjoying myself? Sure, why not?"

"You haven't paid the least bit of attention to the girls Tori invited."

Justin reached for a piece of salmon and sucked it down. He'd gotten used to the raw fish thing at the ranch. His sister was Elk Ridge's assistant chef, and she'd encouraged him to expand his country-boy palate. "I prefer my women with a little more brain power."

Richard laughed. "So do I. Tori's friends are as dumb as she is. Beautiful, but as dense as dolled-up doornails."

"What does Brian see in Tori?" Justin asked, shooting the six-foot blonde a curious glance. She was playing Marco Polo with the kids.

"Empty-headed women amuse him." Richard leaned in close. "They create less pressure than the smarter variety."

"I'll still take the smart ones."

"Me, too. Not that I've had much luck. I've been married and divorced three times." The other man adjusted his glasses. "I heard you were engaged once."

Justin tried not to frown. "Is there anything this family doesn't know about me?"

"We don't know what's inside your soul."

Neither do I, he thought. His emotions were still a mess. "You're different from Brian."

"Easier to talk to?"

And easier to like. Justin didn't want to bond with Richard, but the younger Halloway brother had a way about him. "Is it true that the Hollywood Mob doesn't exist anymore?" he asked, pushing the issue.

"Yes, it is. And the change has been good for me. I was never cut out for that lifestyle. Dad forced it on us. Not all mob bosses do that to their sons. In fact, most prefer to keep their kids out of it." Richard sipped his sake. "But not our old man."

"Why did Brian give it up?"

"Because I got shot and almost died, and he got scared. We've lost a lot of people we've loved over the years, and Brian couldn't take losing me, too. He's more sensitive than he seems." Richard paused. "It was one of those defining moments. When I recovered he just looked at me and said, 'I can't do this anymore.' I knew exactly what he meant. It was over for me, too."

Justin wanted to believe his uncle's story. But Maya sneaking into his room told another tale. And so did his mom's fragile concern. "Is the hit still active on Reed?"

Richard blew out a labored breath. "Dad won't let it go. He's still got connections from prison."

"I don't think I'm going to like my grandfather."

"He wants to meet you. I know this sounds crazy,

but he loves you already. Just being Beverly's boy makes you special. More important than any of us."

Justin angled his head. Had he detected a note of envy? Of rivalry? Or was it pain? "Do you still love him? Even after he forced a violent lifestyle on you?"

"I try." Richard glanced away.

A gap of silence yawned between them.

Then Justin turned and spotted Maya adding more food to the buffet. In the sun, her tightly woven hair glistened with auburn highlights. He wanted to see it loose and free, the way it had been when she'd become his angel.

Damn it. Why hadn't she let down her guard and admited who she was? Why hadn't she whispered it in his ear? No, instead she'd just stood there, staring at him, making his blood rush to his groin. He'd never been this challenged by a woman before.

Richard noticed her, too. "Maya the maid," he mused. "Sleek, sexy, off limits." He gave Justin a serious look. "Do you always want what you can't have?"

"Not before I met her." He needed to find a way to get past this, to be able to talk to Maya out in the open, to earn her trust. "Why can't I have her? What's the big deal?"

"If we get too close to our staff, if we encourage affairs with maids or become bosom buddies with our chauffeurs, we'll invite the wrong kind of employees. We don't want a bunch of groupies or wannabe mobsters working for us. We've always had to be careful not to blur those lines."

"Why does it matter, if you're not involved in organized crime anymore?"

"We're still rich and famous. And we'll always be notorious. The Hollywood Mob will never go away. Not to the media, not to the FBI, not to anyone who doesn't believe that we've gone straight."

"I still want her." Justin wasn't giving up on Maya. No way, no how.

Richard chuckled. "You're a Halloway, all right." He shook his head, sighed. "You'll have to convince Brian to let you have her. He runs this house. He's the boss, and I'm the underboss. That part hasn't changed."

"Then I'll talk to Brian when this party is over. I'll do what I have to do." To be alone with Maya, he thought. To keep his promise.

And keep her safe.

Maya knew she was in trouble. You didn't get called into the boss's office unless you'd done something to displease him.

She headed down the corridor, her sensible shoes squeaking on the black-and-white tiled floor. Mr. B.'s king-of-the-castle lair, with its mahogany furniture and custom-built aquarium, was in the east wing of the house.

Maya knocked, and Brian told her to come in and close the door. She stepped forward. The boss sat behind his massive desk with a holier-than-thou expression. Like Sister Frances, the principal of the Catholic school she'd attended.

Feeling like a knobby-kneed kid, Maya kept her hands at her sides. Sister used to scold her when she fidgeted.

Brian didn't offer her a seat. Out of the corner of her eye, she caught a glimpse of tropical fish.

And then she saw Justin. He stood near the corner of the aquarium. He'd shoved on a pair of threadbare jeans over his swim trucks, leaving the top button undone. His hair, disheveled from diving into the pool, lent him a bad-boy quality.

Rich and spoiled looked good on him. Too good, she thought, scowling in her mind.

Brian finally told her to sit, which she did, taking a chair near his desk. Justin stayed close to the aquarium, enhancing the marine beauty.

"My nephew spoke to me about you," Brian said.

Maya glanced at Justin, but he didn't react, other than to smooth his hair. The ends were still damp.

Nervous, she remained quiet, wondering what he'd said to inspire a nun-type scolding. Unless it was worse than that, unless he'd—

"He wants you."

The room all but tilted. So much for Sister Frances.

"As his mistress," Brian added. "I offered to find him a more suitable lover, but he's quite insistent that he wants you."

Mistress? Lover? The words reverberated in her ears. "Maids don't…"

"No, they don't. Not in this house. But I'm allowing you to become the exception."

Because Justin could have anything he wanted, she thought. Even a woman his family considered taboo.

"If you refuse, you won't be able to work here anymore," the boss told her. "That would be too awkward."

"You'd fire me?"

"No. You'd still have a job. We'd transfer you to one of our vacation homes."

Maya needed to be at *this* location, at *this* mansion, and Justin knew it. She'd told him on the night they'd met.

She glanced at the younger Halloway, but once again he didn't react. He remained quiet, letting his uncle dictate the terms of the indecent proposal.

"Are you attracted to my nephew?" Brian asked.

Her heart pummeled her chest. She wanted to lie, to say no, but she couldn't. "From the moment I first saw him." On the day he'd been kidnapped, she thought, wishing she hadn't gotten herself into this mess.

"Then you'll be with him?"

No, she thought. She wasn't about to sleep with a

stranger, no matter how compelling he was. But if she didn't fake her way through this, she would have to leave the mansion. Not that she couldn't sue the Halloways for sexual harassment. Surely this was a blatant form of it. But suing them wasn't her agenda.

She glanced at Justin. Did he intend for this to be real? Did he expect her to be his lover?

She honestly couldn't tell.

When they were alone in his room, she would set him straight. Maya knew even the best of men could be swayed by sex. And so could cautious women. Her mother had been her father's forbidden lover, a mistress of sorts, and she wasn't about to repeat their mistake.

"Yes, I'll be with him," she lied, trying to sound convincing.

"Then I'll arrange to move both of you to a suite that was designed for couples. It's bigger than the accommodations Justin has now." Brian made a steeple of his hands. "It has a whirlpool in the bathroom. You can enjoy the jets in the tub, Maya. And Justin can take his time and enjoy you."

Her skin turned hot. From anger. From embarrassment. From the image that she couldn't prevent from entering her mind. She knew what suite Brian referred to, but she'd never thought of it as a carnal playground.

Until now.

Brian continued, "There's a lovely kitchen, as

well. And the room next door can be converted into a studio." He angled his head. "For your paintings."

Maya wasn't surprised that the Halloways knew she was an artist. "Did Leo compile a report on me?"

Brian lifted a file from his desk. "We screen all of our employees before we hire them."

Maya didn't respond. She could only assume that Leo hadn't uncovered her true identity. If he had, the Halloways wouldn't have hired her. They wouldn't have trusted Sam Sullivan's daughter. "I've been renting a studio downtown."

"That shabby little place? We can give you so much more than that." The boss turned to his nephew. "Is it all right with you if she continues to paint?"

Justin snared her gaze, making her heart zip. "She can spend her free time any way she wants to."

"As long as she doesn't neglect you." Brian shifted his attention to Maya. "Justin's needs come first."

"I understand." Her art was secondary. Being his whore was her priority. She couldn't think of a more demeaning role to play.

"We'll supply you with a new wardrobe," Brian said. "If you're going to be seen with my nephew, you need to look your best. We'll send you to Tori's stylist to get your hair done, too."

Justin walked over to her. "I want her to wear it long and loose."

Maya took a much-needed breath, and he reached

out to remove her bobby pins and drop them into his pocket. He smelled like chlorine from the pool, like the coconut-scented sunscreen he'd slathered on his skin.

Dizzy, she closed her eyes, wishing Brian wasn't watching, wishing she wasn't on display.

When Justin was done, her hair was a mass of thick, dark waves.

"You're a beautiful young woman," Brian said.

Trapped, she opened her eyes. Justin remained where he was—close enough to make her vulnerable.

"What happens when your nephew gets tired of me?" she asked, knowing their liaison, even a phony one, wouldn't last forever. "When his vacation ends and he goes back to Texas?"

"You can forge ahead with your art career. We're going to help you get established in this town. The perks that come with being Justin's mistress will change your life." Brian closed the file on his desk. "But he agreed to extend his vacation. He isn't in any hurry to leave, so things are settled for now."

"Because they're going to let me keep you." Justin moved in front of her, blocking her from his uncle's prying eyes. "You were the deciding factor."

Steeped in his suntan scent, in his pool-damp proximity, she stood before him like a tortured trophy, grateful Brian couldn't see how uncomfortable she was.

Maya felt as if she'd just sold her soul.

Chapter 4

A duo of maids unpacked for Justin and Maya. The employees seemed uncomfortable. But Justin understood why. They were Maya's co-workers. Until today, they were part of the same household staff, and now Maya was shacked up with the boss's nephew. He supposed it didn't get any more awkward than that.

After the maids left, he got curious and checked out the suite. Located on the first floor, the accommodations offered elaborate sleeping quarters with a canopy bed and a marble, his-and-hers bathroom. The separate living area presented European furnishings, a brick fireplace and a wet bar. A cozy kitchen showcased café curtains and plants on the window-sill. Beyond the breakfast nook, sliding glass doors led to a Mediterranean-style patio with a grass-and-cobblestone yard.

He returned to the living room. The Remington sat in its display case. The statue had been relocated along with his other belongings, creating an illusion that he'd been bought and paid for.

Just like Maya.

She gave him a wary look. She was still wearing her uniform. Lester napped in a pillow-cushioned corner, comfy as could be.

"This affair isn't going to be real." Maya used her fingers, punctuating the count. "No kissing. No foreplay. No sex."

One. Two. Three.

Justin's pride took an instant beating. He hadn't cooked up this scheme to seduce her. But that didn't mean he wouldn't cart her off to bed if she gave him half the chance. She was his angel, his nighttime fantasy.

He couldn't help but want her.

"I know it isn't going to be real," he shot back, hating that she was giving him rules to follow, laying down the off-limits law. "But it was the only thing I could think of so we could be alone. Everyone was making such a fuss when we tried to talk to each other."

"I never tried to talk to you. Not out in the open."

"Yeah, but you started this. You came to my room. You made me promise that'd I help you." A worried thought jumped into his brain. "They might have found us out already. There could've have been a hidden camera in my other room. To keep an eye on me, to make sure I didn't try to escape. It could've been bugged, too."

"It was pitch black when I came in there. They couldn't have seen me. And why would they have bugged it? You were alone. Who were you going to talk to?"

"What about now? This suite could be miked."

"For what purpose? They don't know I'm a threat to them. If they did, they would've gotten rid of me a long time ago."

"You're right. It wouldn't make sense." A knock sounded at the door, and he blew out a heavy breath, annoyed by the interruption.

Maya didn't budge, so he answered it.

Tori was on the other side. The blonde made a sweeping entrance with a ribbon-wrapped basket.

But it wasn't filled with flowers or gourmet food. Justin noticed a generous supply of sensual products, including massage oils, candles and condoms.

Tori set it on the coffee table. "This is so exciting. You and—" She hesitated.

"Maya," Justin provided.

"Yes, the pretty maid." She turned to the brunette

who was supposed to be his mistress. "The basket is from Enamored. I had them send it right over." She smiled. "It's my favorite store. They have lingerie, too. We can go shopping together sometime. I can get you into the VIP room. They serve chocolate and champagne."

Maya didn't respond.

Tori didn't seem to notice. She kept talking to the pretty maid. "You'd look amazing in a sheer corset. Wouldn't she, Justin?"

Did sheer mean see-through? He glanced at Maya, but she avoided eye contact.

He finally answered Tori's question, his imagination doing a naughty number on his libido. "Yes, she would. Look amazing, I mean." He gestured to the honeymoon-type offering and tried to sound casual. "Thanks for the goodies, by the way."

"Anytime." Tori bubbled like the Barbie doll she was born to be. She'd traded her sushi-party bikini for a flamingo-pink dress. "I'll see you guys later."

The blonde left the suite, and Justin glanced at Maya. She still hadn't met his gaze.

Finally she looked at him. "How tacky can Tori be? How can she give us a gift like that? She barely knows us."

Justin shifted his feet. He and Maya barely knew each other, either.

A moment later he glanced at the basket, and his

blood turned warm, heated and hungry. Staying in the same suite with her was going to drive him erotically insane.

He crammed his hands in his pockets and realized that he'd forgotten to close the snap on his jeans. Not that it should matter. He was wearing swim trunks underneath. But somehow, it seemed sexual.

Maya appeared to notice, too. Or maybe she'd been conscious of his jeans the entire time.

He frowned. "I have to get cleaned up."

She nodded, intensifying their awareness.

"We can talk afterward," he told her, anxious to douse his hormones with a pounding spray of water. "And you can tell me exactly why you need my help. Who's missing and all that."

"That's fine," she responded a little too quickly.

Yeah, fine. He turned to walk away, fighting the intimacy between them.

Justin returned from the shower. His freshly washed hair had been combed away from his forehead, but once it dried it would probably fall forward with a mind of its own. Maya was already getting to know little things about him.

He sat across from her, with a rodeo-logo T-shirt and crisp jeans, zipped and snapped. She could have changed, too. But she felt safer in her uniform. Less mistresslike. As fake as their affair was going to be, the intermittent bouts of sexually charged silence made her nervous.

Like now, she thought.

They'd agreed to talk, but no one said anything. She smoothed the hem of her black-and-white dress and noticed there was a run in her panty hose, climbing along her left knee, making its way to her thigh.

Trusting Justin was risky, but since he hadn't turned her over to his family, she could only assume that he was on her side, that he truly intended to help her. Why would he be worried about security cameras and electronic bugs if he were in cahoots with the Halloways?

Finally he cut into the quiet. "Is Maya Reyes your real name? Is that who you really are?"

She took a shaky breath. "Yes, but the Halloways don't know who my father is. His name is Sam Sullivan. Or was Sam Sullivan. I think he's dead now."

"You think?"

Her chest turned tight. "He was an architect, and he disappeared eight months ago." She paused to take another breath. "At the time he vanished, he'd just completed a project for the Halloways. His other family filed a missing person report. I read about it in the paper."

"Okay, wait. Back up. What do you mean, his 'other family'?"

"My dad was married and has three boys who are

older than I am. He and my mom had an affair, but his wife and kids never found out. Nor do they know about me. Mom didn't put his name on my birth certificate, and he didn't pay child support, not in a manner that could be traced. He gave us cash whenever he could. It wasn't a lot of money, though. He wasn't a wealthy man."

"So he was your secret dad?"

She nodded. "It wasn't a typical parent-child relationship, but I loved him, and he loved me."

Justin stood up and walked over to the bar. He didn't ask if she wanted anything to drink. He simply poured two lemon-lime sodas and handed her one.

"It's ironic, isn't it?" He resumed his seat. "The parallel in our lives. The lies, the secrets."

She sipped the soda, suddenly grateful for the refreshment. "I've never told anyone that Sam was my dad. Except you."

His gaze locked onto hers. "You think the Halloways killed him, don't you?"

"Yes."

"Why?"

"Because he disappeared after he worked for them. Even the FBI thinks the mob is involved."

"You talked to the feds?"

"I couldn't. Not without admitting that I was Sam's daughter. But I collected every article I could find. The media jumped all over the federal investigation."

"Did anything come of it?"

"No. But according to what I read, the FBI suspects foul play."

"But they couldn't prove it, so here you are. An artist who went undercover as a maid, who's now undercover as a mistress." He shook his head. "Do you know how crazy this is? If the authorities can't solve the case, what makes you think—"

She cut him off. "I have more at stake than the FBI." Her heart, she thought, the shattered pieces that came with being alone. "My mom died a few months after my dad disappeared, and on her deathbed she admitted that she'd never stopped loving him. Their affair ended ages ago, but he was still the love of her life."

"So you're doing this for your mom?"

"And for me. I need to know what happened to him."

"Maybe the FBI is wrong. Maybe Sam got tired of living a lie. Maybe he needed a break. Maybe he's in the Caribbean somewhere, drinking banana daiquiris and analyzing his life."

"He wouldn't have done that. Not at the expense of the people who loved him. After the affair, he tried to be a loyal husband to his wife and role model to his sons."

"What about you and your mom?"

"He tried to be a good dad to me, too. And a friend to my mom." She put her glass on an end table. "He cared about Mom, but he wasn't in love with her. He was ashamed of the affair. He knew it was wrong."

Justin didn't respond, so she continued, "He met Mom at the hotel where she worked, where she was a maid. He was there for a convention, and they got caught up in each other. He was her first lover."

"How long did it last?"

"A few months. They're both Catholic, so when she turned up pregnant, an abortion was out of the question." Maya thought about her religious roots. "Mom knew the affair was wrong, too. She went to confession. She asked for forgiveness."

"But she still loved him?"

"To her that was the worst part of her sin. Loving a married man. Holding him in her heart all that time."

"I'm sorry, Maya."

"That my mom loved the wrong man or that my dad disappeared?"

"Both." He blew out a rough sigh. "It's got to hurt being his back-street child, staying out of the way to protect his wife and sons."

"I learned to live with it."

"Like I'm learning to live with where I come from?" He ran his hand through his hair. It was already starting to fall forward. "What project was Sam working on? What did he do for the Halloways?"

"He redesigned the wine cellar in this mansion. He added onto the existing structure. He was paid in full and disappeared while it was under construction."

"Have you been down there?"

"The wine cellar? I've pulled bottles for the chef. But I haven't seen the section Dad designed. It's for rare vintages, for the Halloways' private collection. No one is allowed to enter that area except your uncles."

"It's locked?"

"With an alarm."

"It must be some collection." He glanced at the Remington. "Considering how much that bronze probably cost. But smuggling a bottle of wine out the door would be easier, I suppose."

She nodded. "I think so, too. In that regard, the alarm makes sense."

He sat back and studied her. "You can't get into the locked cellar, but you saw them carry me into my other suite? How'd you pull that off?"

"I was hiding in a utility room that has a louvered door. I could see through the slats and hear what they were saying." She explained further, giving him the whole story. "Earlier that day the Halloways called a staff meeting and told us they were reserving the third floor for an important guest and none us were allowed to access that area until they gave us permission."

"So you decided to find out who that special guest was?"

"That's why I got a job here. To watch everything that's going on. Luckily there aren't that many security cameras inside. It's the grounds that are closely monitored. For intruders, paparazzi and whatnot."

"Tell me about the night you snuck into my room."

"There isn't much to tell. I stole a key from housekeeping and returned it before anyone noticed it was missing."

"And now here you are, sharing a suite with me."

She struggled to hide her discomfort. He was looking at her as if he wanted their affair to be real. "I've been here for four months, but until I discovered what they'd done to you, I didn't uncover anything that constitutes a crime. But I don't believe that they aren't mobsters anymore, and I need you to help me prove it."

"What if we prove that they didn't do anything wrong? That they aren't responsible for whatever happened to Sam?"

"But they are," she said, hating that he was giving the Halloways the benefit of the doubt, that he was defending his new family. "I know they are."

"This isn't going to be easy, us picking up where the FBI left off."

Was he changing his mind about helping her? "Then stay out of it, and I'll keep doing it on my own."

"No way," he told her. "No damn way. I'm part of this now, whether you like it or not."

* * *

Later that night Maya locked herself in the bedroom, rummaging through two-piece pajamas and oversized nightshirts.

Justin was in the other room, probably watching the eleven o'clock news. Earlier, he and his uncles had gone to a celebrity-owned restaurant, where Hollywood hard hitters made the scene. Maya hadn't been invited. According to Brian, she wasn't ready to make her mistress debut. To be fair, he'd left Tori home, too.

Not that Tori cared. She'd spent the evening bending Lucifer's ear, planning the menu for the next party, a black-tie event Maya would be expected to attend on Justin's arm.

As his ornament, she thought.

But for now that was the least of her worries. At the moment, she was panicked about sleeping in the same bed with him. She'd considered the sofa, but requesting extra blankets and pillows would call attention to their fraudulent affair.

Finally, she quit digging through the dresser and decided on bright red pajamas. They were the only long-sleeved, long-pants set she owned.

Maya entered the living room, and Justin turned toward her. The gift basket remained on the coffee table like a sex-between-strangers salute. She hadn't known what to do with it, so she'd left it there.

"You look pretty," he said.

"Thank you." She sat on the sofa, and Lester greeted her with a sloppy grin. The dog lay at his master's feet, chewing a rawhide bone.

"You seem innocent," Justin added. "But fiery, too. I never know what to expect."

She glanced at the TV. The weather was being forecast. Heat. And lots of it. "I don't wear sheer corsets if that's what you're getting at."

"But you wear long flowing nightgowns. Or was that my imagination?"

"On the night I crept into your room? That's what I had on." She downplayed her decadence. "Vintage silk. I bought it at a thrift store. That's where I prefer to shop."

"It must be the artist in you." His lips curved into a dimple-beware smile. "The Bohemian."

Was he teasing her? She couldn't tell. Nervous, she warned herself not to fall for him, not to let him shape her into a bad girl.

"What do you paint?" he asked.

"Mexican folk art. *Día de Los Muertos*."

"Day of the Dead?" Apparently he spoke a little Spanish. Or maybe a lot of Spanish. He hadn't revealed that side of himself before now. "You paint those lively looking skeletons?"

"I make *calacas* figurines, too. It's part of my culture, something I was taught to celebrate." *Día de*

Los Muertos was a festive time, where the souls of the departed returned to visit their relatives.

Justin angled his head. "So you're Mexican and—"

"Irish." She thought about her dad and her heart turned sad. "Sam was Irish."

"He could still be alive, Maya."

"He disappeared on All Souls' Day. That might seem like coincidence to you, but it's an omen to me." She'd been creating Mexican folk art before her dad vanished, but now the *calacas* were guiding her.

"I understand," he said, and she remembered that he believed in Cherokee ghosts.

They sat quietly for a moment, lost in their traditions.

"You never told me who the dead baby was," she said, wondering about the infant who'd been buried with a toy identical to his.

He recounted the entire story, and she listened, envisioning the child whose place he had taken.

"Sometimes I paint *los angelitos*," she said.

He frowned. "Little angels? The spirits of dead children?"

She nodded. She could see that he was at odds with the baby his parents had conceived, the child who was their blood. "Maybe I'll paint a *calaca* with a musical pony. Maybe it will bring you closer to him."

"Have you done a painting for your dad?"

"No." Her heart turned sad again. "And I won't. Not until I find out what happened to him."

They didn't speak again, not for a few minutes.

Finally he glanced at the clock. "It's getting late. We should get some sleep."

Her nerves kicked in again. But he was right. It was after midnight.

He stood up and reached for the gift basket.

Her pulse leaped. "What are you doing?"

"Putting this away. We can't leave it on the coffee table forever. But I'll riffle through it first. So when the maids clean the room tomorrow, they'll think we used some of this stuff."

"Yes, of course. That makes sense." She dragged a gust of air into her lungs and followed him into the bedroom. Lester didn't jump up and pad after them. He stayed in the living room in a doggy bed that had been provided for him.

Justin went through the basket, jostling the contents, then storing it in a walk-in closet. When he turned around the impact of his gaze nearly swallowed Maya whole.

He went into the bathroom to get ready for bed, and she waited, listening to the water run. She'd already brushed her teeth and washed her face.

A short while later, he returned without most of his clothes. All he had on was a pair of pinstriped boxers.

His sleeping attire, she thought.

"Which side do you want?" he asked.

"It doesn't matter. I move around a lot."

"You're a restless sleeper?" He turned down the bed. "So am I. But look at this romantic monstrosity. There's got to be enough room for both of us."

Romantic monstrosity? She studied the cream-and-gold comforter, the corded edges on the pillow shams, the elegantly draped fabric creating the canopy. "You're right. We should be able to survive it."

He flashed his dimples. "Unless you roll over on top of me. Then I'll have to restrain you."

With what? The braided ties on the canopy? The fuzzy handcuffs in the gift basket? "You have a rotten sense of humor, Justin."

The dimples deepened. "Okay, fine. You can restrain me instead."

Good Lord. She grabbed a pillow and swatted him with it. Or tried to swat him. He ducked, missing her swing.

They both laughed, realizing how idiotic their situation was. But by the time they climbed into bed and turned off the light, a veil of seriousness settled over them.

Intensifying the affair that wasn't supposed to be real.

Chapter 5

The next morning Justin awakened in the center of the bed, with Maya right next to him. He had no idea how long they'd slept so close together, but if she really were his mistress, he would pounce, jump her so fast her pretty little head would spin.

She opened her eyes, and they stared at each other. Her night-siren hair was strewn across a pillow, and the buttons of her pajama top strained across her breasts.

He reached out to touch her cheek, and she flinched. He wondered what she would do if he leaned in to kiss her.

Probably call him a cheat. Or a liar. Or a Halloway.

Justin dropped his hand. He'd had girlfriends. He'd had lovers. He'd even had a fiancée. But he'd never had a mistress.

Frustrated, he sat up and leaned against the canopy frame. She sat up, too. But she moved away from him, making him feel like a bastard. Because he wanted her as his mistress. He wanted her at his beck and call.

The phone on the nightstand chimed, screaming into the morning. He grabbed it on the first ring. "What?" he said.

"Trouble in paradise?" came the smart-aleck reply.

Leo, he thought. He recognized the security chief's gruff voice. "What do you want?"

"To give you a message. Your uncles request your presence in the garage."

"When?"

"At ten o'clock. Oh, and bring your virgin bride."

Justin glanced at Maya. Leo assumed she was a lousy lay.

The other man chuckled, enjoying his own wit.

Justin hung up, summoning yet another reason to punch Leo in the mouth.

At ten o'clock, Justin and Maya arrived at the garage. He hadn't told her how cynical Leo was, but she was astute enough to figure out the gist of it on her own, making their relationship even more awkward.

He wondered how they were going to pass themselves off as torrid bedmates, let alone find out what had happened to her father.

The massive garage doors were open, revealing a fleet of cars. Justin's truck was among them.

Footsteps sounded, and he and Maya turned simultaneously and saw his uncles. Brian boasted impeccable posture and a fine-tailored suit, and Richard looked as average as ever. But billionaires didn't have to be suave, Justin thought, getting a mental image of Bill Gates.

A dark form caught his eye, and he noticed that Leo had showed up, too, standing in the background, creating a wide shadow.

Brian moved forward, addressing his guests. "Good. You're right on time."

"Yes, we're here." Justin reached for Maya's hand and held it briefly, creating a moment of morning-after intimacy.

Or so he hoped.

She turned toward him, and they gazed at each other. When they broke eye contact, Justin glanced at Leo. The security chief didn't react.

"We come bearing gifts," Richard said.

"Yes, we do." Brian gave Justin and Maya each a set of keys. "Would you like to guess which cars are yours?"

"Aside from my truck?" Justin went along with his uncles' game, seeing how much it pleased them.

There were at least twenty vehicles on display, including a long black limo. But he knew instantly.

"What do you think?" Justin asked Maya.

"I don't know." She seemed uncomfortable about accepting a fancy new ride from the Halloways. But apparently it came with being a mistress.

Justin divided his gaze between Brian and Richard. "It's the Porsches. The 911 Turbos. They're the only cars without license plates."

Brian flashed a rich man's smile. "But whose is whose?"

"Hers is red, mine is silver."

"Give the boy a gold star." Richard winked at him. "And some gold cards to go with it." He handed Justin a MasterCard, a Visa and an American Express. He gave Maya the same plastic trio. She almost dropped hers.

Justin thanked his uncles, offering handshakes, but they both reached out to hug him instead.

The unexpected affection threw him off kilter, especially coming from Brian, a man who normally kept his emotions at bay.

He wanted his uncles to be innocent, to be free of the crime Maya believed they'd committed. But he knew they could have Sam's blood on their hands.

Maya finally played her part, managing to thank them, too. Justin imagined it was the most difficult thing she'd ever done.

Brian's warmth was short-lived. He took charge, telling Maya that he'd planned her day, scheduling a meeting for her with a fashion stylist who would help her shop for a new wardrobe. After that, she had an appointment to get her hair and nails done.

Before she climbed behind the wheel of her 911, Justin grazed her lips with his. It wasn't exactly a kiss, but it was mouth-to-mouth contact, and it made her shiver. He noticed the quaking effect.

He was certain that Leo noticed it, too. But he wasn't sure how the security chief had interpreted it.

As she drove away, Richard said, "She looks good in red."

Justin agreed, thinking about the pajamas she'd worn last night.

Brian added his opinion. "I told the salon to add more red to her hair. I think it'll suit her."

From there, he excused himself, claiming he had work to do. Leo disappeared, too.

Justin and Richard were left at the garage.

"Did Brian pick the Porsches?" Justin asked. The way he'd made a personal decision about Maya's hair... Not that Justin hadn't done that, requesting she wear it long and loose, but she was supposed to be *his* mistress, not Brian's.

The other man frowned. "You don't like the make, model, color? You want to trade yours in for something else?"

"No. I just wondered if there's anything Brian doesn't control."

Richard shrugged and then smiled, as if his brother being in charge didn't bother him. "You'll get used to it."

"Will I?"

"Sure. Come on, there's something important I want to show you."

They entered the mansion, and Justin considered his uncles. Were they playing the bad boss/good underboss routine purposely? Was it part of their Hollywood Mob dynamics? Something they'd always done? Or was there something else going on? Something Justin was missing?

And what about Leo? Just how much clout did he actually have? How important was he to the Halloway dynasty?

"This way," Richard said, leading him into a den with an old-fashion vibe.

A pinstriped sofa, a Windsor chair and a pine coffee table complemented a Norman Rockwell painting. Family portraits cluttered another pastel wall. In the center of the framed photographs was a poster-size picture of a young woman wearing a lavender dress and a soft smile.

"That's your mother," Richard told him. "That's Beverly. It was taken on her eighteenth birthday. She died four years later."

Justin studied her image. Her honey-blond hair swept her shoulders, and her eyes were an emerald shade of green.

"She was beautiful," he heard himself say.

"Yes, she was. I think your father fell in love with her the moment he saw her."

Justin didn't want to think about Reed, but curiosity got the best of him. "So you believe that he loved her? That what he felt was real?"

"Yes." The other man paused. "Brian prefers to pretend otherwise. But he knows it's true."

"Were you friends with Reed?"

"No, but I admired him at first. He was bright and charming. The kind of guy who got everyone's attention." Richard met his gaze. "You're a lot like him."

The comparison struck a chord. "No, I'm not."

"Yes, you are. But that doesn't mean you'll try to destroy us the way he did."

Guilt hit him hard and fast, and he struggled to temper the fist-to-gut reaction.

Richard kept looking at him. An unblinking stare. Then he said, "She died of cancer."

Justin shifted his feet. "What?"

"Your mother. She got small-cell carcinoma. Lung cancer. It's rare in someone so young, but it happens." Richard sighed. "Without treatment, it can kill someone within two to four months."

"Is that how quickly she passed?"

His uncle nodded. "And she didn't even smoke. How ironic is that?"

Justin gazed at Beverly's picture again and realized how empty her smile really was. "Was this taken before she met Reed?"

"Before he stole her away from us? Yes, it was." Richard walked over to a rolltop desk and lifted the wooden slats. He removed a piece of paper. "We'd like you to fill this out."

"What is it?"

"A visitor's form to see your grandfather in prison." Richard moved closer, holding out the white sheet. "The department of corrections will have to screen your application. It'll probably take a few weeks, and Dad's already chomping at the bit to meet you."

Justin took the form, his stomach twisting into a mobster-driven knot. He didn't want to visit his grandfather, but Denny could be the one who'd made Sam Sullivan disappear. He remembered Richard telling him that Denny still had connections.

"He'll probably cry when he sees you," Richard said.

Justin couldn't picture the patriarch of the West Coast Family getting misty-eyed. He didn't envision Denny as a frail old man. "Does he cry when he sees his other grandchildren?"

"No. But you're different. I already told you how much he loves you."

"He loves the idea of me."

Richard handed him a ballpoint pen. "Beverly was his favorite. His only daughter. Dad would've died for her."

Justin sat in front of the coffee table, preparing to fill out the form. His uncle's voice had gone flat, the way it always did when he discussed Denny.

"What happened to your mom?" Justin asked. "To my grandmother?"

"She passed away when we were kids. Dad kept mistresses after that. There's been a lot of women in and out of this house."

Like Maya, Justin thought, wishing he wasn't hungry for their affair to be real.

And wishing the Halloway blood wasn't running so deep within his veins.

Maya returned from her shopping expedition, went straight to her suite and found Justin on the patio, playing fetch with Lester.

Undetected, she stood back and watched them, man and dog, enjoying the late-afternoon sun.

Lester caught the ball in midair, spun around and saw her. Like the big rambunctious puppy he was, he dashed through a carefully tended flower bed, trampling the foliage to bring her his prize.

With the ball still stuck in his mouth, he jumped up and pawed her new outfit, smudging the breezy fabric.

She took his toy and threw it, knowing Justin had caught sight of her, too. She could feel the heat of his gaze.

He came toward her, and she told herself to relax, to fight the self-consciousness.

"Damn," he said.

"I know. I look different." Her hair had been fluffed into long, auburn-streaked layers, and a sizzling summer dress clung to her curves. Strappy shoes and bold jewelry accessorized the Beverly Hills ensemble. Even her undergarments, a pushup bra and skimpy thong, were new. As for her legs, they were freshly waxed and bare. Her bikini line had been waxed, too. Modesty hadn't been part of her day.

He wouldn't quit staring. "You look incredible."

The humiliation got worse. She dusted away the dirt the dog had left on her dress. "The stylist picked this out. She chose all of my clothes, telling me what I had to buy."

"I like it. *Really* like it." He reached out to touch her hair. "And as much as I hate to admit it, Brian was right."

She didn't ask him what he meant. She assumed he was talking about the forced highlights in her hair. "The rest of my wardrobe is being delivered. And these nails…" She lifted her hands. "They're supposed to be a professional length. But I think they're too long."

"They're perfect," he countered.

For what? Clawing a man's back? "They're fake."

"Yeah, but those white tips are classy. I've always been into that."

"You have?" She frowned at him. "Since when do cowboys care about French manicures?"

He shrugged, laughed a little. "I was raised on a five-star guest ranch. It's like a Hilton with horses. I got used to that kind of stuff."

Lester barked, interrupting their conversation. They'd both forgotten about the dog. He'd come back with the ball, waiting for someone to throw it.

Justin tossed the toy, then returned his full attention to Maya. "Don't be upset with how they made you look. It works on you."

"But I'm not even allowed to wear panty hose anymore. The stylist says they're not sexy. Either my legs have to be bare or I have to wear those thigh-high kind that stay up on their own." She made a pained face. "Or a garter belt. How cheesy is that?"

He made a pained face, too. "What are you trying to do? Torture me?"

"That isn't funny."

"I'm not kidding." He looked straight at her. "You're my walking-talking fantasy."

Confusion hit her hard and quick. She envisioned pawing him like a cat. Or shredding his shirt with her dice-and-splice nails.

Earlier when he'd brushed his mouth across hers, she'd gotten all sleek and shivery. And now she was standing before him as the Molotov cocktail his family had created.

"You're messing with my emotions, Justin."

He didn't back down. He stayed where he was, close enough to touch her, but keeping his hands to himself. "You're messing with mine, too."

Then why didn't their attraction seem fair? Why did it seem as if he had the advantage?

Because he did, she thought. A mistress was starting to emerge. Somewhere in the pit of her shamed soul, she knew how sultry she was bound to become. That sooner or later, she would enjoy the sinful feeling.

Lester barked, but no one tossed the ball this time. The dog finally gave up and chewed the rubber, snubbing the couple caught in the throes of each other.

"I'm not sleeping with you," Maya said, warning Justin, cautioning herself.

"You already told me that yesterday."

"So I'm telling you again."

He lifted her chin. "You're not very convincing."

"And you're acting like one of them."

"One of who? My uncles?" He stepped back, squinted, steeled his expression. "No one can seem to make up their mind. Either they tell me I'm a Halloway or they tell me I'm like Reed."

She had no idea what kind of person Reed was,

but she admired him for putting Justin's grandfather behind bars. "What am I supposed to think? You offered to help me, but you haven't."

"I made you my phony mistress."

"That wasn't the kind of help I was looking for."

"I'm working on finding out what happened to your dad."

"Are you?"

He gave her a tight nod. "We're going to the kitchen to request a fruit and cheese platter from the chef."

She angled her head. "What for?"

"So we can pick out the right vintage to go with it. I want to check out the wine cellar."

"We won't be able to get into the secured area."

"Not now. But I've got a plan for that."

"Then let's go," she said, anxious to see what he had up his sleeve.

Grateful the tension had passed, Maya walked beside Justin, taking a sconce-lit hallway and veering off to the kitchen.

The chef's assistant, a middle-aged woman who didn't let Lucifer get under her skin, was working on a shopping list. She glanced up and did a double take, checking out Maya's chic ensemble. Then she offered a genuine smile.

Lucifer wasn't so accommodating. He greeted the new Halloway heir with, "What can I do for you, sir?" and behaved as if Maya wasn't there.

"We'd like a fruit and cheese platter sent to our room," Justin responded.

"May I recommend strawberries, grapes and melons with an imported French Brie?"

"I don't know." Justin turned to Maya, forcing Lucifer to acknowledge her. "What do you think?"

"Include kiwi," she told the chef, thinking how good it felt to give him an order. "And a Camembert spread with neutral crackers."

"Certainly." His impeccably trimmed goatee twitched, but he finally made eye contact, treating her with the same respect as her supposed lover.

"We'd like some wine, too," Justin said.

"Of course." Lucifer shifted his gaze. "I'll provide you with a list. We catalog our wine by taste."

"That won't be necessary. I'd like to browse the cellar instead."

"Our inventory is quite extensive. Perhaps a list would—"

"I don't want a list. I want Maya to give me a tour of the cellar." Justin sent the other man a condescending smile. "So I can steal a kiss between the racks."

Lucifer cleared his throat. "That's your prerogative, sir."

"You bet it is." Justin took Maya's hand. "Care to lead the way?"

"It would be my pleasure." The kiss, she hoped, was part of Justin's ploy to make sure they weren't interrupted and not something that was actually going to happen.

With her heels echoing on the floor, Maya directed Justin to a set of terra-cotta-tiled stairs. They made the descent and entered the wine cellar.

Stained glass art provided churchlike color, and the racks, fashioned from Honduran mahogany, staggered in height and structure, branching into hallways and cavernous corners.

"Is any of this new?" he asked.

"No. It was built with the house." They walked between rows of wine-enclosed wood with trellised pigeonholes, cubes, rectangles and diamond-shape niches. "The only addition is the part my dad designed."

"Where is it?"

"Here." She took him past the tasting room and into an area with a locked door and sophisticated keypad.

"So this is it? The end of the line?"

She nodded. "It's as far as we can go."

"Then let's grab some wine and put the rest of my plan into action."

She studied him. His dimples surfaced, then disappeared, playing peekaboo with a half-cocked smile. "Which is?"

"You'll see."

Ten minutes later they chose a Sauvignon Blanc that would complement the snack they'd ordered. Justin seemed fairly schooled in wine selection, and she assumed his knowledge came from being raised on that five-star guest ranch. The classic choice would have been red Bordeaux, but he believed that pairing crisp white wine with fatty cheeses was far more interesting. And Maya agreed.

Without so much as a hint of a kiss, they returned to the kitchen and handed Lucifer the bottle.

"Excellent choice," the chef said. He was in the midst of preparing an artfully designed platter, arranging the fruit and cheese just so.

Justin snagged a strawberry and handed it to Maya. She bit into it, knowing how Lucifer hated it when someone disturbed his masterpieces before they were complete. Apparently Justin knew it, too.

"I'd like to see the private wine collection," he said, getting the chef's attention once again.

Lucifer looked up. "I'm sorry, sir. But I don't have access to it."

"Then call Leo and tell him to get his ass down here."

The chef did Justin's bidding, and Leo showed up in record time, expecting a security breach. But what he got was the Halloway golden boy insisting that he wanted to view the private collection.

"May I ask why?" Leo asked, dressed in his usual dark suit.

"I'm a wine enthusiast," Justin responded.

"Really? I didn't know that."

"Well, now you do."

"It's not about the wine," Leo challenged. "You just don't like being locked out."

Justin squared his shoulders. "You're right, I don't. So talk to Brian about giving me the alarm code. And quit treating me like a second-class citizen. I'm a valued member of this family. I've got a brand-new Porsche and a pretty girl to prove it." He paused, furthering his point, reminding the security chief that he'd been a key player in Justin's kidnapping, a federal offense that Justin had chosen not to report. "Positive DNA results, too."

Leo wasn't pleased. A muscle ticked in his jaw, but he agreed to speak to the boss.

Maya stood her ground, as well. Being Justin's mistress had its advantages.

They returned to their suite and congratulated each other on a job well done, anxious to eat, drink and enjoy their victory.

As dusk textured the sky and melded into shape-shifting clouds, Justin and Maya shared a mosaic table on the patio. Citronella candles burned, and Lester begged off their plates.

"This is nice," Maya said.

Justin nodded. He liked being outdoors, but he liked being with her even more.

She lathered a cracker with the Camembert spread

she'd ordered and gave it to the dog. The pooch gobbled it right up. "The maids call him Lucifer."

He made a face. "My dog?"

She laughed, reached for another cracker. "The chef."

"Oh, him." Justin laughed, too. "He's an ass."

"So is Leo."

"He's the one who's demonic. I don't trust him."

"Me, neither." Her mood turned serious. "Do you think he's involved in my dad's disappearance?"

"I don't know." He sat back in his chair. His plate was still filled with festively carved fruit. "Tell me more about your investigation. Has anyone at the mansion said anything useful?"

"You mean other employees? It's a tight-lipped group. Aside from frivolous gossip now and then, they keep their mouths shut. Tori blabs, but I've never heard her put your family in a bad light."

He leaned forward. "Did you do an online search?"

"That's where I got most of the articles I mentioned before. If you Google Sam's name, a bunch of stuff comes up about him being missing and about his connection to the Halloways."

"Did he do any other jobs for them?" Justin asked, trying to make sense of the murder she thought had been committed. "Or just the addition?"

"That was it." She paused to sip the Sauvignon Blanc. "But wine cellars were his specialty."

"Did the Halloways use a contractor who specialized in cellars, too?"

"Your uncles own a construction company. It's one of their businesses. Why? Do you think it matters?"

"You said Sam disappeared while the addition was being built. Maybe that's a piece of the puzzle." But Justin couldn't be sure. He wasn't a cop. He'd never had to solve a crime.

She looked up. "Do you know anything about construction?"

"I remodeled a couple of rooms in my house. I could've hired a carpenter, but I wanted to do it myself. I like building things." He tasted his wine. "Did your dad work for any other prominent people?"

"He designed a cellar for Kane Carter."

"The actor?" Justin let out a low whistle, catching Lester's attention. "Mr. Number-One-at-the-box-office?"

She placated the dog, giving him another treat. "Kane is friends with your uncles. I think he recommended Sam. I think that's how Dad got the job."

"Have you seen Kane's cellar?"

"No, but Dad told me he designed it." She frowned at him. "It was a few years ago, when Kane was working on that Renaissance movie."

"Is Kane a private collector? Does he have a secured area, too?"

"I don't know." Her frown deepened. "Are you accusing my father of designing something other than wine cellars? Of being involved in something illegal?"

"I'm just exploring all the angles."

She gave him a pointed stare. "He was a good man."

"Sometimes good people get mixed up in bad things."

"I know. But Dad getting caught up in something criminal doesn't fit his personality."

"And keeping you a secret does? Not telling his wife and sons that he had a daughter?"

"That isn't the same thing."

"Neither of our families is perfect."

"Yes, but yours is dangerous." She made an exaggerated gesture, pointing out the obvious. "They're trying to seduce you."

He took in his surroundings, cursing the rich-and-famous allure. He was knee-deep in his uncles' world. But so was she. "Listen to you. The lady whose art career is going to be boosted. We're both in danger of being seduced."

"It scares me, Justin."

He reached out, linking their fingers.

She closed her eyes, and he lifted their joined hands and pressed his lips to her skin. She opened her eyes and looked at him.

"I almost got married once," he heard himself say.

She blinked. "To who?"

"A girl from my hometown." He recalled his engagement: the department-store china pattern they'd chosen, the house they'd intended to build, the kids he'd assumed they were going to have. The full-blown lie he'd been living. "At the time, I was trying to be more like my parents. More settled. More white-picket fence." He glanced at the sky. Dusk had turned to night. "But I'm different from them." Restless, he thought, the way Brian accused him of being.

"I'm different from my parents, too. Or I'm trying to be different from my mom." She took her hand back. "I don't want to get mixed up with the wrong man."

"You mean me? It's too late for that. You already are." They'd collided from the instant she'd become his angel, from the moment he'd awakened, drugged and confused and sensing her presence.

She shivered, even though the evening air was warm. "It'll be over when we prove that my father was killed."

"And that my uncles did the ghastly deed?" His muscles tensed. "I'd much rather find him alive."

"Me, too." Her eyes turned misty, and she struggled not to cry. "But that isn't going to happen."

Justin didn't argue with her. He simply accepted her grief.

And absorbed it as his own.

Chapter 6

Another day. Another damsel-in-distress dilemma.

The nights were tough, but mornings were getting the worst of Maya. After what? Less than a week?

She glanced at Justin. He was still asleep, the covers bunched around his waist.

She wanted to move closer, to smooth his rumpled hair, to experience his day-old beard stubble, to awaken him with an erotically charged kiss. But she knew better.

Not that she was inexperienced. Even good girls had sex these days. But Maya didn't have short-term affairs. She didn't tumble into lust-driven liaisons.

Even if she wanted to, even if that was what Justin instilled in her.

Before she did something stupid, she climbed out of bed and went into the bathroom to take a shower.

As she removed her oversize T-shirt, she frowned. The stylist had chosen sexy nightgowns for her, but since she didn't have to pretend to be Justin's mistress when they were alone at night, she wasn't about to wear them. She did, however, toss them into the laundry basket now and then to fool the maids, to make them think she liked looking hot for her man. She and Justin had to keep up the pretense that they were lovers.

Maya closed her eyes. The shower did little to cool her I'm-falling-for-him heels. The water beaded on her naked body, heightening the feeling.

Finally she dried off and grabbed her robe. Justin's was draped next to hers, and it smelled faintly of his cologne. His-and-hers intimacy, she thought.

After applying makeup, blow-drying her hair and curling it, she returned to the bedroom and rummaged through her side of the walk-in closet. She ignored the erotic gift basket Justin had stored on his side and reached for a hanger.

She got ready in the dressing-room-sized closet, zipping into a retro-style jumpsuit and adjusting a wide leather belt, an accessory that had been chosen to go with it, at her hips. Stilettos came next. Already her feet were crying for relief.

But she and Justin wouldn't be holed up in their suite all day, and his family expected her to wear the man-pleaser fashions they'd provided.

She exited the closet and examined her image in a full-length mirror, adding geometric jewelry.

"You look like Emma Peel," a rough voice said from behind her.

She spun around and saw a gorgeously groggy Justin checking her out. As he sat up, the covers dropped below his waist, exposing the elastic on his boxers.

"*The Avengers,*" he clarified.

Maya took a Heaven-help-me breath. "I know who you're talking about."

He dragged his sleep-tangled hair off his forehead, combing it back with his fingers. "She's my favorite secret agent. I've got *The Avengers* DVD collection at home. The newer movie was cool, but I like the old TV show better."

"That's probably why I was railroaded into this outfit. Brian probably told the stylist to make sure I got an Avengers type jumpsuit."

"Probably." He sent her a sinuous smile. "I always wanted to do her. Emma, I mean."

Good Lord. "Mrs. Peel was married."

"Yeah, but her husband was a test pilot who was lost on a mission and presumed dead. He came back, though."

"See. I told you she was married."

"You're not." He patted the bed. "Wanna spar with Mr. Steed?"

It would be more like sparring with a stallion, she thought. "Very funny, Justin."

"Can't blame a guy for trying." He got up and put on a pair of jeans. A moment later he sauntered into their cozy kitchen to brew some coffee. "Do you want a cup?" he called out.

"Yes, thank you." She was tempted to make the bed, but she knew a maid would be cleaning their room later. Still, the romantic-looking disarray was tough to bear.

A few minutes later, Maya accepted the coffee Justin offered, adding nonfat milk and a sugar substitute. He dumped a massive amount of powdered creamer into his. His family knew how he liked his coffee. They made sure the kitchen was stocked with his preferences.

She studied him, trying to figure him out. "What was your fiancée like?" she asked, wondering what sort of woman he'd almost married.

"She was the girl-next-door type, I guess. That's what I was looking for at the time. What I thought I wanted."

"What was her name?"

"Claire."

Country Claire, Maya thought, envisioning her as bright and pretty. "How did you meet her?"

"A mutual friend introduced us. The engagement lasted about a year. I bailed right before we sent out the invitations." He glanced at his cup, focusing on the lightened liquid. "She'd already ordered her dress and all that."

"You must have broken her heart."

"I prefer to think that I saved her from disaster." He looked up. "Besides, she's with someone else now."

Suddenly a nail-pounding sound caught his attention. The noise was coming from the room next door.

"They must be working on your studio," he said. "Do you want to check it out?"

She agreed, and they took their coffee with them.

Richard was overseeing the job, making sure the two-man crew built shelves for her supplies and constructed an impressive worktable. Adjustable easels had been provided, too. And bigger windows were being installed.

Richard turned to Maya, telling her how lovely she looked. Then he said, "I hope you're happy with the renovations."

"Who wouldn't be?" It was the kind of work space she'd always dreamed of having. But she hated herself for liking it.

"I'm glad you're pleased." The underboss smiled. "As you know, we're hosting a black-tie party on Saturday. The manager of our gallery will be attending, so you can meet him then."

Justin interjected. "You have a gallery?"

"Art is one of our passions. And our business endeavors. But I'm sure Maya already knows that."

"Yes, I do." Prestigious patrons and Hollywood posers flocked to the Melrose Avenue establishment, intrigued by its mobster-glam owners.

"I'm looking forward to getting acquainted with your work," Richard told her. "Our exhibition program balances emerging and mid-career artists with those who are already established. You should fit right in."

She merely nodded, wishing once again that she hadn't gotten herself into this mess.

"Who inspired you?" he asked, continuing their conversation. "Who's your favorite artist?"

She had a ready answer. "Frida Kahlo."

"Ah, yes, of course. The famed Mexican painter." He paused, pursed his lips. "All those haunting self-portraits. Who wouldn't be captivated by her?"

The pounding in the room rattled the walls, and everyone fell silent.

Finally Richard turned his attention back to Justin. "I heard that you spoke to Leo about the wine cellar."

"That's right, I did."

"Your mother always wanted to collect rare wine, so we chose the collection specifically for her, vintages she expressed an interest in."

"Really?" Justin squinted at his uncle. "Leo didn't mention that."

"It wasn't his place to tell you."

"You or Brian could have told me before now."

"We meant to. But we wanted to take the time to explain the whole story to you. The architect who designed the cellar disappeared. We didn't have anything to do with whatever happened to him, but there was a nasty federal investigation."

Maya tried to not react, to weave on her feet. Justin, as always, kept his cool.

"The FBI blamed the Hollywood Mob," he said.

"Exactly," his uncle responded. "Nothing came of it, but Dad was so upset, he thought we should've stopped construction on the cellar. He thinks the architect disappearing taints the wine collection. Brian and I weren't sure if it would affect you the same way."

"It doesn't matter. I'd still like to see it. Even more now that I know it's connected to my mother."

Richard sighed. "That's good. Brian will be relieved, too. You can get the code from Leo today. He isn't on duty yet, but he'll be in his office in about an hour. It's in the security suite, on the third floor, past the theatre."

"Thanks. I appreciate that."

"We'd never lock you out of the wine cellar or anything else." The older man reached out to touch his nephew's shoulder. "You're one of us. And you always will be."

* * *

Justin and Maya returned to their suite, and she looked as if she could barely breathe.

"I never expected Richard to say anything about my dad," she said.

"Me, neither. And I didn't expect the wine to have anything to do with my mom. That bit about my grandfather threw me, too," he admitted. "But Richard being up-front about the federal investigation makes sense. Why would my uncles try to hide it? Considering it's public knowledge."

"I know. But it still made me nervous."

"You did good. You didn't let it show."

"I tried not to."

After that, a stream of awkwardness passed between them. But that always happened when their conversations faltered. Emotional tension, Justin thought. Sexual awareness.

He arched his back, stretching his muscles, working out the anxious kinks. "Since we have an hour to kill, I'm going to take a shower."

She nodded, and he walked away. He intended to linger over his daily routine, but he blasted the water instead. Preparing to face the rest of his day, he got completely dressed, adding a denim shirt and lace-up boots to the jeans he'd had on before.

Finally he joined Maya in the kitchen where she was keeping busy, watering a plant on the window-sill. He moved closer, and they both glanced at the clock on the wall. It was still a bit too early to see Leo.

"Where are the articles you've been collecting about your dad?" he asked. "Where do you keep them?"

She put the pitcher down. "In a safe deposit box at the bank. I didn't want to take the chance of trying to hide them here." She looked tall and shapely in her tight clothes and spiky heels. "I did the research at an Internet café. I had to pay to print the documents, but I figured using their computers was safer. You know, rather than having it traced back to mine."

He managed a smile. "You really are Emma Peel."

"A secret agent?" She smiled, too, but it didn't reach her eyes. "It's starting to seem that way. For both of us."

"I suppose it is." He paused, curious about her. "What did you do before this? Besides your art? How'd you make a living?"

"I worked for a caterer."

He smoothed his shower-damp hair, pushing the jagged pieces away from his eyes. "So that's what helped you land the undercover kitchen maid job?"

"I think being raised by a maid helped, too. Mom's work history probably came up in the background check Leo did on me."

Since there was coffee left in the pot, he refilled his cup from earlier and added more powdered creamer. "What about your dad?"

"What about him?"

"If Sam's name isn't on your birth certificate, then whose is?"

"No one's. It says that my father is unknown."

"Is that common?"

"Common enough, especially if you're illegitimate."

He was illegitimate, too. But he didn't want to think about the circumstances of his birth. Plagued, he drank his coffee, needing the caffeine boost. It had taken him hours to fall asleep last night. Sharing a bed with Maya was catching up with him.

Finally he put his empty cup in the sink. "It's about time. Are you ready to get this show on the road?"

She nodded, and he could tell that she was nervous again. The secret agent was faltering.

"I'm finally going to see the addition Dad designed," she said. "Thank you for helping me. It means a lot."

"You're welcome." He leaned into her. He wanted to give her a passionate kiss, to open his mouth against hers. But he didn't. He pressed his lips to her forehead.

Sweet and vulnerable, she skimmed his cheek. "I was wrong. And so is Richard. You're not one of them."

"Maybe not." He stepped back, putting a deliberate distance between them. "But I like the turbo-charged car they gave me. And I like having a mistress."

"Even a fake one?"

"That part is difficult. I can't help but want this to be real."

"Sometimes I do, too," she said. "But I know I shouldn't."

Now he really wanted to kiss her, to push their attraction to the brink. But he guided her to the security suite instead.

Justin and Maya announced their presence and waited to be buzzed in. Leo and several members of his staff viewed surveillance monitors, keeping an eye on the mansion.

The Hulk rose to the occasion, getting up and out of his chair, cynical as ever. "What took you so long?"

Justin gave him a cool stare. "Don't screw around. Just give me the code."

"I plan on it." Leo didn't comment on Maya's sexy makeover, but he gave her a quick roam with his eyes. Then he motioned to his private office, a room adjacent to the monitors. "You can come in, but the lady will have to wait here."

"That's fine." Justin hadn't expected her to be part of the numbers exchange. "But I'm bringing her with me when I view the wine collection."

"As long as you don't give her the code. It's supposed to stay within the family."

After Justin let go of Maya's hand and entered Leo's domain, the other man closed the door.

"It's quite a few digits, but you'll have to memorize it," Leo said. "You can't write it down."

"I've got a good memory."

"I'll bet you do. You're probably a genius like your old man. Traitor that he was."

Justin refused to tense, to let his emotions show. "I don't even remember Reed. He's nothing to me."

"Yeah, but you know what they say. Blood is thicker than water." Leo paused. "It's thicker than wine, too."

"Apparently my uncles think so."

"Because they built the cellar for your mother? Expect to see some security cameras."

Damn it. He cursed in his mind. He didn't want to be filmed, not while he and Maya were checking out the area Sam had designed.

"There are other cameras in this house," Justin said, trying to seem unconcerned.

"Not that many." The Hulk went into his smart-mouth mode. "And not in such tight quarters. You might not be able to hide your bad side."

"I don't have one," Justin responded, refusing to let Leo best him. "And neither does Maya. Maybe we'll give you a show, and you can see how hot we are for yourself."

"I'm not interested."

"You won't watch?"

"No."

"Really? You're not a voyeur?" Justin mocked. "All it takes is one camera for that."

"Funny guy." The Hulk mocked him right back. "Keeping track of what goes on around here is my job. Oh, and one more thing. Don't touch the wine. Don't mess with the bottles."

"Why not?"

"Because if you break one, it'll be my responsibility to replace it. To hunt down another bottle. Protecting that collection is part of my job, too."

"God forbid I should make more work for you."

"Just follow the damn rules," Leo snapped.

"Whose rules? Yours? Or my uncles'?"

"Both. Do you know how difficult those wines are to find?"

Justin didn't respond. Frustrated, he got the numbers, then turned and left, taking Maya with him.

As Justin and Maya descended the cellar stairs, she exhaled a quaking breath. Would she feel her dad's spirit? Or would the locked room seem empty?

Like a corpseless coffin, she thought, getting a chill. She hesitated on the last step, and he turned to look at her.

"Are you okay?" he asked.

She resumed walking. "I'm just glad you're here with me. I don't think I could do this alone."

He didn't say anything, but he reached for her hand, lending his strength, his support. Much like this morning, she wanted to kiss him, to press her body against his, to let him sweep her away. But once again, she knew better. Nothing had changed since then. She hadn't summoned Justin's help to get tangled up in an affair.

They kept moving, silence between them.

"Ready?" he finally asked.

She nodded. She knew he was talking about entering the locked cellar. By now, they were there.

"Stay close to me when we're inside," he told her. "So we can whisper. In case the cameras have audio. I doubt they do, but…"

She agreed, and he stepped forward and disengaged the alarm. An electronic door opened and they crossed the threshold.

"I hope we don't get trapped in here," she said, keeping her voice hushed. The entryway was dimly lit with shadows bouncing.

"Don't worry about it. There's a keypad on this side, too."

She walked beside him, staying as close to him as possible, and when they came to the main room, they both stopped and stared.

"It's beautiful," he said.

"The architecture? Yes, it is." She wanted to touch everything, but she wasn't about to call attention to herself on camera.

The room itself was fairly small with a Spanish tiled floor, an engraved archway and an antique table. A graceful mahogany rack showcasing seven bottles of wine took center stage.

She couldn't feel her dad's spirit, not in a physical sense. But his ghost hovered in her heart. She recognized the style of his work. She'd seen pictures of other cellars he'd designed.

Maya turned toward Justin, and they continued to whisper.

"I expected the collection to be bigger," he said.

"Me, too. But look over there." She indicated an empty display rack, an entire wall with wooden pegs and vacant slots. "Maybe they're going to add to it. Maybe the other vintages they're looking for are even harder to find."

"I don't know much about rare wines."

"Me neither."

He took her hand and moved closer to view the collection. "We'll have to do some research."

"I wonder how valuable they are."

"I don't know. But we need to remember what they are."

"Instead of asking Leo to make us a list?" She glanced up. The security cameras were in plain sight. "Should we wave to him?"

Justin glanced up, too. "Maybe we should flip him the bird." He smiled a little. "I told him that we might give him a show."

She blinked. "What?"

His smile dimpled. "For the cameras."

Her heart nearly stopped. He meant a sexual show.

Touching, kissing, teasing. "That's not funny." Her skin turned warm. "You shouldn't have said something like that."

"I couldn't help it. Leo pissed me off." He heightened their whispered conversation. "By the way, I'm glad you admitted how you felt about me."

That pretending to be his mistress was difficult? That deep down she wanted it to be real?

She struggled to keep what was left of her virtue intact. "That was a mistake."

"No it wasn't." He slipped his arms around her, then pressed his mouth directly to her ear, making the moment even more intense. "But the first time I kiss you isn't going to be in front of Leo or anyone else. When it happens, I'm keeping you all to myself."

With that, he released her and studied the collection some more. So did she, with her pulse pounding and her concentration wavering.

Finally, he led her to the keypad and opened the door, leaving those seven bottles behind.

Chapter 7

Maya and Justin left the mansion, and she rode shotgun in his new Porsche. They were headed to Charlie's Web, the Internet café she frequented, to do some research. She'd already given him directions.

Before she got sidetracked, she removed a pen and paper from her purse and started scribbling.

"What are you doing?" he asked.

"Writing down what was in the wine collection. Or trying to. I only got two of them, and even then I'm not sure."

He sped in and out of traffic as if he'd lived in

L.A. his entire life. "It doesn't matter. I know what all of them are."

"You memorized everything? The name of each winery? The year? The grape variety? The whole bit?"

"Yes."

"That's amazing."

He stopped at a red light. "It was only seven bottles."

"I know, but it'd be easy to mix them up. Are you sure you've got them straight in your head?"

"I'm sure."

She put away her pen and paper. "What are you? Some sort of genius?"

He scowled at her. "Don't call me that."

"Why not?"

"Because I got it from Reed."

She shook her head. "Would you rather be dumb?" She made an air-brain face. "Like Tori?"

He gave her an exasperated glare and punched the car into gear when the light changed. She thought he should be proud of his gift. But she bit her tongue, letting him stew in his own smarts.

They drove in silence the rest of the way.

When they arrived, he nabbed a parking space on Santa Monica Boulevard and turned toward her. She looked at him, meeting his gaze and wondering why he hated seeing his father in himself.

Was it because Reed's character was always under fire? Or because he'd let his baby son go?

"I'm sorry," he said suddenly. "I shouldn't have taken that out on you."

"It's all right." She was tempted to touch him, but she didn't. "We have a lot going on. The last thing we need to do is argue."

He agreed, and they took to the sidewalk.

Charlie's Web was an eclectic eatery where out-of-work actors, starving artists, desperate musicians and unsold screenwriters often gathered, seeking misfit solace. A variety of soups, salads and sandwiches made up the menu. If you weren't interested in getting online, you could play complimentary board games.

They entered the building, and Justin looked around. "Interesting place," he said.

She nodded. With her skin-tight jumpsuit and his hunky cowboy gear, they blended right in. Together they made a beeline for the last unoccupied computer, located across from a boy with blue hair and a girl wearing imitation leather.

Blue Boy and Pleather Girl were playing Scrabble, spelling out undetected words. The tables were far enough apart to afford privacy.

Maya went up to the counter to order lunch, and Justin started the research. When she returned with the food, he was immersed in his task.

She sat beside him and noticed how Internet savvy he was. Justin *was* smart, she thought. Book smart.

Street smart. She'd heard that geniuses often lacked common sense and sensitivity. She didn't know if it was true, but it didn't define Justin. His emotional intelligence seemed superior, too.

"Any luck?" she finally asked.

"First of all, rare wines aren't as costly as I thought they'd be. According to what I've uncovered so far, the most expensive bottle of wine ever sold was from Thomas Jefferson's cellar, with Th. J. etched in the glass. It went for a hundred and sixty grand. It's too old to be drinkable, though. Someone who collects Thomas Jefferson memorabilia bought it."

"What about the wines your family has?"

"They're all drinkable. The current value is about fifteen to twenty thousand a bottle. It's a good collection. Very good."

"Are they as rare as Leo claimed? As difficult to replace?"

His expression was tense. "It wouldn't be impossible to replace them, but yeah, it'd be a pain hunting them down. There aren't that many in existence."

"Then why do you seem skeptical? What's wrong?"

"The more I think about it, the more it bothers me that I'm not allowed to touch them. Wine that's associated with my mother? Why would anyone think that I'd be that careless as to break one?"

"Maybe the collection doesn't have anything to do

with Beverly. Maybe they're using that as some sort of sentimental excuse to overly protect it."

"That's what I'm thinking." He frowned at the monitor. "What if there's something else in those bottles? Something more valuable than wine?"

Her imagination kicked into gear. "It could be drugs. Something in liquid form."

He disagreed. "Seven bottles would be a pretty paltry smuggling operation."

"What about diamonds or something like that?"

"I don't know. But those bottles could be the key to all of this."

To her dad's disappearance, she thought. To his murder. To everything she'd loved and lost.

"I think I should get some sort of audio jammer," he said suddenly. "Something that will protect our conversations."

She thought about how they'd whispered in the cellar. "Are you still concerned about them bugging our suite?"

"With the way I lock horns with Leo? The guy in charge of the phony wine collection? Or whatever the hell it is? If anyone gets suspicious of us, it'll be him."

Maya wasn't about to disagree, not this time.

Justin went back to the keyboard and did an online search of countersurveillance equipment. "Here we go. Check this out. They even make portable jammers to carry in your pocket. I can get one of those, too. Then we don't have to worry about being bugged in other parts of the mansion, either."

"Like the wine cellar?" She studied the screen, then hesitated for a moment. "Didn't Reed build those types of devices for your family?"

He frowned. "Yes. But they're sold commercially because a lot of corporations use them. I'll make sure I get top-of-the-line stuff. No cheap gadgets. We need the real deal." He frowned again. "Like Reed used to build."

When he turned away from the screen to look at her, he touched her cheek, giving her a tender chill.

"I'm not like him," he said, referring to his wayward father. "I'd never run from my responsibilities."

"Do you feel responsible for me, Justin?"

"Yes," he told her, making her realize how much she needed him, how important they'd become to each other.

On Saturday evening, Maya got ready for the black-tie party, putting the finishing touches on her appearance. She donned a strapless, shimmering white gown that hugged her breasts and flared at her hips. Her hair was half up and half down, styled in a purposely messy chignon.

As for the environment, it was safe from electronic eavesdropping. As promised, Justin had purchased high-dollar devices that desensitized microphones, putting them in well-concealed places throughout the suite.

"You look incredible," he said.

"So do you," she told him, her heart skipping a girlish beat. He wore a modern three-button tuxedo with a satin lapel.

He stepped forward. "I have something for you." He handed her a small velvet box. "I wanted to give it to you before you put on any jewelry."

"Is it for me to wear tonight?"

"Yes, but it's from me, not the Halloways. I didn't buy it with any of their credit cards. It has nothing to do with them."

She opened the box and saw an antique gold locket, decorated with an ivory rose and dusted with diamonds. She nearly lost her breath. "Thank you. It's beautiful." An ornate treasure she never expected.

"It's from the Victorian era. I figured you'd like it because it was old, and you're into vintage stuff. But I wanted you to have it because of the rose."

"Why?" she asked, gauging the seriousness in his voice.

"White roses are associated with the Trail of Tears, the journey the Cherokee made when they were forced to migrate. They had to leave their homeland because gold was discovered."

She glanced at the necklace and waited for him to continue.

"They traveled during the winter," he said. "And nearly half of the people died along the way." He paused, then explained further. "The young mothers wept because they couldn't save their children. So the elders called upon the Creator, praying for a sign that would lift the mothers' spirits and give them strength. The next day a white rose with a gold center began to grow wherever a mother's tears had fallen."

She pressed the velvet box to her chest. In her mind's eye, she could see his ancestors, leaving tear-formed flowers in their wake. "Did the gold center represent the gold that was taken from their land?"

He nodded. "There were seven leaves on each stem, too. One for each clan."

"What clan are you from?"

"I thought it was the Paint Clan. But it might be different now."

Because he was Reed's son, she thought. And some of the things he knew about himself had changed. But even so, he was holding on to his heritage and inviting her to be part of it. The way she'd invited him to be part of hers when she'd offered to paint a *calaca* of the baby his parents had buried.

She met his gaze. "This is the most special gift anyone has ever given me."

"I can't take credit for the idea. I'm not the first man in my family to give a woman something that represents a Cherokee rose. My great uncle started the tradition."

"You've never mentioned him before."

"His name is Bobby Elk. He raised my dad. Michael," Justin clarified, letting her know he wasn't talking about Reed. "Bobby also built the guest ranch where I grew up."

She smiled. "The Hilton with horses?"

He smiled, too. "That's the one."

Maya held out the necklace to him. "Will you help me put this on?"

He agreed, and she turned around. He clasped the chain, his breath warming her skin.

"I never gave my fiancée anything that represented a Cherokee rose," he said. "I should have, I guess, but I didn't. Considering she was the girl I was going to marry."

Maya faced him once again, and an emotional firefly zapped between them. She felt like a bride in her glittering white gown and romantic locket.

"Why me instead of her?" she asked.

He glanced at the ivory flower. "I don't know. It's just something I was compelled to give you. To do." He lifted his gaze and looked into her eyes once again. Warm, tender, intense. "Are you ready to go?"

"Yes." She fought another bride-type feeling and accepted his arm, allowing him to escort her.

The party was in the ballroom. Elegantly designed, it offered a polished oak bar, a separate buffet room and a sweeping dance floor. French doors led to the garden.

In the past, Maya would have worked an event like this. But here she was, arriving on the guest of honor's arm.

Twinkling lights and organza-decorated columns presented a stunning effect, while a three-tiered fountain filled with balloons created a focal point. A tuxedoed band crooning Rat-Pack-era tunes lent the soiree a men-rule-the-world-and-women-are-broads flair.

Mack the Knife and martinis, Maya thought. It fit the Halloways to a T.

Brian approached them, shaking Justin's hand and kissing Maya's cheek the way he did with other female guests. He wasn't singling her out.

The boss introduced Justin to Hollywood CEOs, real estate moguls, investment bankers, cosmetic surgeons, high-profile attorneys, recognizable celebrities and do-nothing heirs. Maya was introduced, too. No one seemed aware that she used to be a maid. That she'd served them appetizers before.

Justin was disappointed that Kane Carter, the actor Sam had built a wine cellar for, hadn't made the guest list. But Kane was on location, making a movie. Maya wasn't sure if Kane was relevant. From what she'd read, the FBI had already cleared him of any wrongdoing, eliminating him as a suspect in Sam's disappearance.

Tori came up to Maya and gave her a hug. They

weren't the only glamour girls there. The ballroom overflowed with trophy wives and girlfriends.

The blonde wore a fuchsia gown that plunged from her neck to her navel, with thigh-high slits up the sides.

"Wow. Look at you," Maya said.

"You, too." Tori admired Maya's dress, then zeroed in on her necklace, reaching out to examine it. "That's Victorian."

"Yes, it is." Surprised, Maya angled her head. She hadn't expected the other woman to be an antique jewelry connoisseur. Her tastes seemed more modern. Then again, Tori sometimes wore vintage Tiffany.

"In those days, women used to carry around a lock of hair or a photograph," the blonde said. "That's why most Victorian pendants and brooches have lockets on the backs of them." She paused. "Did Justin give it to you?"

Maya nodded, wondering if he would think it was odd if she asked for a snippet of his hair to keep inside the rose. She glanced in his direction. He was standing a few feet away, conversing with a director immortalized on Hollywood's Walk of Fame.

"Do you think men like them ever marry women like us?" Tori asked.

Maya knew she was talking about Brian and Justin, not the sidewalk-star director. "I don't know."

But the question made her uncomfortable. She'd already been foolish enough to feel like Justin's bride. "Do you want to marry Brian?"

"Yes, but I shouldn't. I know he cheats on me. I've even confronted him about it."

Maybe Tori Tell All wasn't as dumb as she seemed. "Are you in love with him?"

"Desperately. But I shouldn't be thinking about this right now. I have a party to host."

Within the blink of an eye, Tori flitted off to greet other guests, leaving Maya wondering about her.

But she didn't have time to contemplate Brian's leggy lover for long. Richard brought Hutch Fielding, the gallery manager, over to meet her, then left them alone to talk shop.

Hutch sent her a charming smile. In his mid-to-late forties, he stood tall and straight, with brown hair, graying temples and blue eyes.

"You're as enchanting as your work," he said.

Maya met his gaze and got hit with nostalgia. Hutch reminded her of her dad. Not his appearance. They didn't look anything alike. But his personality, his easy manner, made her homesick for her childhood, for the stolen moments she'd spent with Sam.

"You've seen my paintings?" she finally asked. "My figurines? I didn't think you'd be familiar with them yet."

"Actually I've been aware of you for quite some

time. After the Halloways hired you, Leo told me about you."

She tried to seem unaffected, but knowing that the security chief had talked about her didn't sit well. "Because I was an artist moonlighting as a maid?"

He nodded. "I got curious and researched your work. You're good, Maya. Exceptionally so. But I couldn't have offered you a show then. The Halloways wouldn't have allowed me to promote one of their maids."

"But it happened anyway."

"Yes, it did."

He finished his cocktail. A skewered olive remained in his glass. He twisted it between his fingers, turning it like a top. Her dad used to toy with garnishes, too.

"It's strange," he said. "The way things turned out."

Stranger than he knew, she thought.

"Are you friends with Leo?" she asked, hoping that he wasn't.

"I don't think it's possible to be friends with Leo, not with that attitude of his. But I've learned to tolerate him." Hutch finally ate the olive and discarded his glass on a bar-height table. "Sometimes he consults at the gallery. On security issues." He shook his head and laughed. "Not on the art."

She relaxed, and a moment later Justin glanced over and became aware of her easy rapport with

Hutch. He ended his conversation with the Walk of Fame director and moved to stand beside Maya.

The men introduced themselves, shaking hands and locking gazes.

"I'm going to schedule a show for your lady," Hutch told Justin. "I'm looking forward to giving her the recognition she deserves." He turned to Maya. "I'll be in touch." He waited a beat and noticed Justin's possessive stare. But he didn't drop his smile. "It was a pleasure meeting both of you. But I should mingle. There are a lot of art collectors here."

He walked away, and Justin watched him go, escorting Maya to a quiet corner so they could talk without being overheard. "I don't like him."

"I do," she admitted. "He seems sincere. Especially after what he said about Leo's attitude. Besides, he reminds me of my dad."

Justin frowned. "What do you mean?"

She repeated her conversation with Hutch, mentioning his Samlike mannerisms. But Justin wasn't impressed.

At this point, Maya thought he was behaving like a jealous lover. Even if their affair wasn't real, even if he still hadn't made good on his promise to kiss her.

He reached for her, staking his claim and making her forget about Hutch. "I don't want to fight."

Her heart bumped her chest. "Neither do I."

"Then dance with me. Let me hold you."

Maya glanced at the stage, where the lead singer crooned a soulful tune.

She agreed to dance, and the song put them face-to-face, swaying to a retro rhythm. They moved naturally together, hands properly positioned, bodies in sync.

They weren't the only couple out there, but they summoned the most attention. Justin's family made a point of watching, and their interest drew other glances.

The Halloway golden boy was making the most of his party, letting everyone know how much he appreciated his mistress.

As the song ended, as the final lyrics faded, he brought her straight into his arms and leaned in to kiss her.

Her pulse leaped. "You said you didn't want to do that in front of anyone."

"I changed my mind." His mouth captured hers, and she held on for dear life, clutching his shoulders and forging a hot, hard bond.

It only lasted for a few seconds, but the rest of the evening went by in a blur. She ate; she drank; she socialized. But she couldn't stop thinking about the desperate taste of him. She knew he was obsessing about her, too. She could see it his eyes.

So why fight it? Why sleep in the same bed every night and not touch each other? Maya needed to be caressed by him, to feel his body imprinting hers.

Justin was more than the man determined to help her.
He'd become a friend, a confidant, a should-be lover.

An affair that was meant to be real.

Maya was nervous. But she did it. Heaven, how
she did it.

Later that night, with Justin as her captive audi-
ence, she unzipped her dress and stepped out of the
shimmering fabric.

Entranced, he watched her. "You should feel how
fast my heart is beating. You should feel what you're
doing to me."

She released a pulse-pounding breath. She was
seducing him. Yet she was being seduced, too. He
couldn't take his eyes off of her.

And why not?

She stood before him in a strapless bra, lace
panties and a matching garter belt, with silk stockings and three-inch heels.

Already her skin was flushed. Modeling sexy
undergarments was as foreign as a French lesson, but
removing them took every ounce of courage she
owned. She started with her bra, opening the hooks
and exposing her breasts.

"I fantasized about this," he said, making hot and
cold chills rush her spine. "The color of your nipples,
the darkness of your—"

He was tripping over his words. But she could tell

that he wanted to lick and suck and make her melt in his mouth.

Like rock candy. Like a boyhood treat.

She drew a breath. "What else have you fantasized about?"

He dropped his gaze. "Seeing you down there."

Maya almost swayed on her feet. He was waiting for her to ditch her panties, to toss the lace aside. But her shoes and stockings and garter belt were in the way, so she got rid of them, her hands trembling in the process.

He spoke to her in Spanish, calling her his beautiful angel. Nervous, she pushed the delicate panties down her hips, giving him what he wanted.

What they both needed.

He took his gift, and then some. He moved forward, swept her into his arms and carried her to bed.

Enthralled, she arched to kiss him. He thrust his tongue in her mouth, over and over, making the moment last. He tasted like the classic martinis he'd drunk.

Gin, vermouth and an elegantly tuxedoed man.

Only the tuxedo didn't last long.

He removed his tie, threw his jacket on the floor, kicked off his shoes and ripped open his starched white shirt, barely leaving his pants intact.

"You better not regret this afterward," he said. "You better not wonder what the hell you did."

"You either."

"Are you kidding?" He gave her a rakish smile, his dimples flashing, his charm brimming. "I'll want to do it again. As many times as I can."

She sank deeper into the bed. He was putting his hands all over her, and she'd never felt more alive.

More sensual.

He went after her nipples, licking them like sugared peaks. She shivered, and he moved lower, making circles with his tongue, leaving cool wetness on her stomach.

Justin Elk was dangerous, and she damn well knew it.

But she wouldn't regret being his lover. She wouldn't go to church and confess him as a sin. It was too late for that. A higher power couldn't save her.

He put his mouth between her legs, and she clawed his scalp, watching every thing he did, climaxing hard and fast.

When it ended, he rose up to kiss her. "We're going to need that basket."

"For a condom?" she asked, bumping his fly.

He pushed back, his pants grazing her skin. "Maybe some of the other stuff, too."

She went warm and wet all over again. "You're corrupting me."

Yes, Justin thought. He was. But he couldn't help it. There she was, erotically naked, looking as luxurious as the cream-and-gold comforter that surrounded her. The only thing she wore was the Cherokee rose.

He retrieved the basket and placed it in the middle of the bed so they could pick through it.

"You can choose the type of condom you want," he told her.

She opened a variety pack. "Some of these are flavored. That might be fun."

He nixed the idea. "Those aren't for the real deal."

She fisted a packet that said Kiss of Mint. "What if I want to do to you what you just did to me?"

He went unbelievably hard. Already his zipper was straining. "You can't. Not right now. I want this to last."

"Then you pick the condom."

He grabbed a ribbed style. And some candles and massage cream.

She seemed pleased with his romantic choices. He put the basket aside, lit the candles and turned off the light. The wax began to melt, scenting the room with a floral aroma.

"That's perfect," she said.

"So are you." He poured lotion into his hands and rubbed it on her body, making her even softer and silkier than she already was.

She removed the rest of his clothes and did it to him, too. And by the time she closed her fingers around him, his heart banged against his chest.

He pulled her onto his lap and kissed her. He

thought about her rules. No kissing. No foreplay. No sex. All of it was happening. They were breaking every single one.

And he couldn't survive another second without being inside her.

Justin tore open the condom and used it. Then he shifted positions.

She wrapped her legs around him, and they went desperate-for-each-other mad. He thrust full hilt, and she bit her nails into his shoulders, leaving catlike marks.

He loved every hungered sensation, every torrid feeling. Beats of thunder echoed in his veins, and he buried his face against her throat.

Sweet, sultry Maya.

Justin thrived on the physical connection, on lifting his head and taking her mouth in a tongue-tangling kiss, in the jagged force of possessing her.

They rolled over the bed and she landed on top of him, riding his arousal.

He circled her waist and increased the motion. The pins had already fallen from her hair, sending the dark strands spilling onto her shoulders.

The driving rhythm didn't stop. Not for an instant.

He looked into her eyes. Her body tensed, and he knew she was going to come. Two times in one night. She was his fantasy, all right. Everything a man could dream.

Justin couldn't hold on. He came, too.

After it was over, after he discarded the condom, she snuggled against him.

He held her, even if he was still half hard, even if he hadn't quite lost his edge. It wouldn't take much for him to do it again.

"I'm not good at this part," he said.

She cozied up some more. The cat had gone kitten. "You're doing fine, Justin."

He stroked a hand down her hair. "We could relax in the tub if you want. Turn on the jets."

"I haven't soaked in the tub yet," she admitted.

"Why? Because of what Brian said? I could tell that he embarrassed you."

"I'm not embarrassed anymore. Not after what we just did."

"Then let's indulge in some water therapy." Recalling a product he'd seen earlier, he reached for the basket and removed a bottle of Sexy Bubbles. "We can use this."

She looked at it and laughed.

He laughed, too. Then he read the label. "It's supposed to make the water feel velvety." He popped the cap. "And it's supposed to have an intoxicating aroma."

She took a whiff. "That's nice. Mild."

He nodded, grateful it was designed for couples. He didn't want to smell like a girl when they were done. "My sister uses scented stuff in her bathwater. She always puts it on her birthday list."

"Do you buy it for her?"

"Every year. She's specific about what she wants. You know what I want?" he asked, changing topics. "To see you in a see-through corset."

"I have lots of lingerie, Justin."

"I know, but I can't get that out of my mind."

She smiled, climbed out of bed. "Then I'll have to get one."

They went into the bathroom, filled the tub, turned on the jets and added the Sexy Bubbles. From there, they sat across from each other.

They'd brought the candles, too. The flames flickered, dancing in the dimly lit room.

"Now I'm glad Tori gave us all that stuff," she said.

"So am I." He leaned over to kiss her, then sat back, thinking how pretty she looked with water silhouetting her body, with the tips of her breasts—

"She wants to marry Brian."

He blinked. "What?"

"Tori. She's in love with him."

"Then maybe you should get to know her better. Maybe she'll give you a better insight into what he's really like."

"If he's still a criminal? You know he is."

"I keep hoping he isn't. And Richard, too."

"Are you getting attached to your uncles?"

Was he? Even after they'd kidnapped him? Even after they'd insisted that he meet his grandfather? Even after he suspected the wine collection was bogus? "I can't help it. I don't want them to be as bad as they seem."

She didn't respond.

In the silence, one of the candle flames vibrated, making an ominous shape on the wall.

Worried that he'd spoiled the moment, he flicked water at her, trying to coach a smile between them.

She splashed him back, and soon they were kissing and touching like the lovers they'd become.

The Halloway heir and his mistress.

Chapter 8

The following morning Justin and Maya were summoned by the great and powerful boss. Seated in the formal dining room with white linens and fresh flowers, they had breakfast with Brian, Richard and Tori.

Richard poked at his plate, frowning at the gourmet selection.

Brian treated his younger brother like a child. "If you don't like your meal, order something else."

"It isn't the food. I'm tired and hung over. I would have preferred to stay in bed." He glanced at Justin and Maya. "They look whipped, too."

Justin didn't say anything. If they were whipped, it was because they'd made love three times last night and again this morning. He couldn't get enough of Maya. He couldn't stop touching her.

Brian gave them a serious study. "They look just fine to me." The boss smiled a little. "Besides, breakfast is the most important meal of the day."

Richard rolled his eyes, turning away so his brother couldn't see him.

Justin almost laughed. He couldn't help but like his second-in-command uncle. Richard never seemed to let Brian get to him. Besides, it did seem crazy to drag their party-weary, sex-exhausted butts out of bed to eat quiche and scones and yogurt. The coffee was the only thing Justin gave a damn about. But when Brian said frog, they all jumped. That was how the Halloway dynasty was run.

The boss put down his fork. "Actually I called everyone together because I have some news. I got a call from Dad's attorney this morning." He turned to Justin. "Dad is adding your name to the title. You'll have to sign some papers, but—"

Justin cut him off. "The title of what?"

"This house."

Damn. He knew he was an heir, but he hadn't expected to be offered a portion of the mansion. "Who else is on it?"

"Dad, Richard, David and me."

"David?" The name didn't ring a bell. "Who's he?"

Brian responded again, "Our oldest brother. Your other uncle. He was the boss before I took over."

"His picture is in the den," Richard interjected. "I thought I pointed him out."

"No, you didn't." But there were lots of family photos in the den. The pictures spanned multiple generations. "Why haven't I met him?"

"He's in prison." The boss resumed eating, but his posture tensed.

"For what?" Justin asked, although deep inside he knew.

"Murder. His mistress turned him in. She went into witness protection after that."

Like Reed, Justin thought.

"I'll bet it was difficult for her," Tori blurted. "Betraying the man she loved."

Brian frowned, and Justin met Maya's gaze, an unspoken look passing between them.

Richard broke the silence. "You haven't met David's daughters yet," he said to Justin. "They spend their summers abroad."

Curious, he sat back in his chair. "Who's their mother?"

"David's wife. She stood by his side. In fact, she put a hit out on his mistress. More out of power than jealousy. David's wife wanted to run the West Coast family, to take David's place, but Dad wouldn't hear of it. Women aren't allowed to wear the crown."

"What about David's children?" Justin asked.

"What about them?" Richard parroted.

"Is my grandfather adding their names to the title? Or any of my other cousins?"

"No." This came from Brian, who handled the rest of the conversation. "The mansion has always been owned by men. Richard and I have daughters, too. But you know our girls."

Justin nodded. He'd been introduced to them at the pool party and had seen them again last night. They were older than he was, married with kids of their own. "Is this about gender? About me being Denny's only grandson?"

"Yes, but not in the way you think. Dad doesn't want his granddaughters being associated with what the media calls the Mob Mansion. He gave them their own houses. He would have done that for your mother, too."

Justin raised his eyebrows. "What does that make me? One of the mob?"

"To Dad, it does." Brian finished his quiche. "But it doesn't matter because that part of our lives is over."

"So I'm a token mobster?" Christ, Justin thought. Could this situation get any worse? Could he be falling any deeper into his grandfather's web?

"It's easier than being the real thing," the boss said. "Believe me, I know."

"Me, too." Hung over or not, Richard finally decided to eat. "And I'm glad I'm free. That both Brian and I are."

After breakfast, Justin and Maya went for a walk in the garden, taking Lester with them. The dog had a field day, sniffing flowers and plants. He chewed a few roots, too, digging them out of the ground.

Justin corrected him, even if the gardeners would repair the damage, even if no one seemed to care if his puppy ran wild.

"I wonder if good old Grandpa will put Lester on the title, too," he said, as the dog squatted to pee.

Maya sighed. "He'll probably have to learn to lift his leg first."

"Yeah, to be a man." He turned to look at her. "Did you already know about David and his mistress?"

She nodded. "I researched the entire family before I came here. I read about David and Nancy in old newspaper clippings on the Net."

"Nancy?"

"Nancy Perris. That was her name back then. But it would've been changed once she went into witness protection."

Justin studied his surroundings, thinking how surreal the Mob Mansion was. He and Maya stood near a mermaid fountain, watching water trickle from seashells. "Did you come across any pictures of Nancy?"

"Yes." Maya walked away from the fountain. "She had dark hair."

"Like you?" He followed her to the rose garden. She was still wearing the ivory flower he'd given her.

"We actually look kind of similar. Or we did in the pictures I saw. She would be a lot older than me now."

"So I have the same taste in women as David? I hope they don't want me to visit him in prison. He's not eligible for parole, is he?"

"No. And neither is your grandfather. They both got determinate life sentences."

"Grandpa conspired to commit a murder, and David committed one. They're quite a pair. Lord only knows how many other killings they were involved in that they got away with." He heaved a heavy sigh. "Last night you asked me if I was getting attached to my uncles. I am. To Richard, anyway."

"I can tell that you like him. That you want to be able to trust him. But in some ways, he creeps me out more than Brian."

He frowned at her. "Why?"

"Because he seems so nice. So normal."

"Like the gallery manager who reminds you of Sam?" The pebbled path crunched beneath his shoes. "That's creepy, too."

"It is, isn't it?" Her voice cracked. "I just miss my dad so much."

"I know. I'm sorry."

They continued walking among petals, leaves, stems and thorns. "I should befriend Tori today," she said. "I should try to get inside her head. Mistress to mistress," she added, her voice going gravelly again.

He reached out and took her in his arms. "We're not like them." He blew out an unsteady breath. "Are we?"

"You mean Brian and Tori? And David and Nancy?" She put her head on his shoulder. Her breathing was shaky, too. "I don't know."

"Neither do I." Justin held her, deep and close, immersed in their affair.

In emotions they couldn't begin to describe.

Maya and Tori took the limo to Enamored, the lingerie store where Tori had gotten the gift basket. As they rode in the long black car, Maya studied the other woman, who was decked out in leather and lace.

Not that Maya looked like Sister Frances. She sported her fair share of flash, too.

"How did you meet Brian?" she asked, initiating a personal conversation.

Tori answered the question with ease. But she hadn't been nicknamed Tell All for nothing. "I worked as an exotic dancer at one of the West Coast Family clubs."

An alarm bell went off in Maya's head. "Isn't that what Nancy Perris used to do? Isn't that how she met David?"

Tori sighed. "She auditioned, but I don't think she ever danced. Brian closed down the clubs after he quit being a mobster. There was too much bad stuff going on that he couldn't control."

"So you believe that Brian isn't a criminal anymore?"

"Yes, I do," came the solemn response. "He helped me get off drugs."

Dang. Maya hadn't expected that. "You were an addict?"

The blonde nodded. "Coke, crystal, crank, you name it, I did it. I didn't live a very nice life when I was young. Neither did Nancy. She more or less came from the streets, too. But David didn't save her. Brian told me that David used to manipulate her."

"But she loved David anyway?"

"He was all she knew. She'd been with him since she was a teenager."

"And that's why you said it must have been difficult for her? Turning David in?"

"Yes. But mostly I said that because I'd have to do the same thing to Brian if he started being a criminal again. I got involved with Brian when I was struggling to get clean, and he was disbanding the mob. We seemed right for each other. Two people trying to better themselves."

Maya was beginning to like Tori, to appreciate her, but she didn't know what to think of Brian. Had he made a legitimate effort to go straight? Or was it a scam? A facade to commit criminal acts under the guise of being good? "I just hope he doesn't hurt you."

The blonde frowned, pouting her plumped-up lips. "He already is. I shouldn't put up with the other women. But Brian refuses to make a commitment to me. Not that he was faithful to his wife. I was with him when he was married. I probably deserve this."

Maya thought about her mother. She'd had an affair with a married man, too. "No one deserves to be hurt."

Tori made a mock gesture, showcasing the limo, indicating her sleeping-with-a-billionaire perks. "At least I get to spend his money."

"That you do."

Silence settled over them until Tori asked, "Are you falling in love with Justin? Do you want to be with him for the rest of your life?"

Suddenly Maya couldn't breathe. She couldn't monitor the oxygen that was supposed to be fueling her lungs. "I haven't known him for very long."

"People can fall in love right away."

"I'm not that type."

"I think you are. I think you're dreamier than you're willing to admit."

Dreamier? She'd never even used that word before.

The car stopped, signaling their destination. The driver got out and opened the door, escorting both women onto the Walk of Fame. Enamored was located on Vine Street, two blocks south of Holly-wood Boulevard. Maya didn't glance down to see whose five-pointed pink star she'd stepped on. She'd quit doing that when she was a kid. She still remembered where Snow White's star was, though. She hoped that didn't make her *dreamier*.

They entered Enamored and Tori led Maya to the VIP room. While they shopped, they sipped high-dollar champagne and nibbled on gourmet chocolate.

Tori was addicted to lingerie. These days, baby dolls, bodysuits and bustiers were her drugs of choice.

Maya headed toward to a rack of corsets. She found a sheer style made of white mesh and deco-rated with gold ribbon. A pair of matching panties went with it.

Maybe she and Justin were like the other couples. Like Tori and Brian, she thought. Like David and Nancy.

Powerful men. Women eager to please.

Her shopping companion glanced over. "That's pretty."

"Justin wants to see me in one of these." Even if he'd already seen her naked, even if he'd touched and kissed every part of her. "But you put the idea in his head."

"It doesn't take much to put those kinds of ideas in a man's head. Ohhh, look at this." Tori grinned. "Chain mail."

"Metal underwear?"

"It'll make me look medieval." The blonde handed her items to a salesgirl, who'd already started a purchase pile on the counter. Tori didn't try anything on. She just bought whatever she wanted. "Let's check out the costume section."

Curious, Maya followed her, catching sight of schoolgirl uniforms, lady-cop outfits and naughty nurse dresses.

"You have to get this." Tori grabbed a French maid getup, fashioned from vinyl and slit up the back for bending over. "Tell me how perfect it is for you."

"No way. I couldn't—"

"Oh yes you can." Tori thrust it at her, and they both laughed.

But in the end, Maya bought it.

Because the maid turned mistress couldn't resist.

Maya returned to the mansion and put her packages in the closet. This wasn't the time to entice Justin with her purchases. He was waiting to hear about her conversation with Tori. So she told him. Not the misguided love part. Not the *dreamier* stuff. She only repeated the dialogue that involved his uncle.

"So do you think Brian is on the level?" he asked.

"I don't know." They sat across from each other in the living room of their suite, the ever-present de-bugging devices protecting their conversation. "What he did for Tori was honorable, helping her get off drugs. But it's ironic, too. The West Coast Family is known for drug trafficking. The person your grandfather conspired to murder was a drug dealer who'd cheated them. David killed a different dealer. And Richard was shot in a transaction gone bad. They're mired in it."

"Richard said it was the shooting that put them on the straight and narrow. That him almost dying was what changed their lives."

"If your uncles aren't criminals anymore, then who made my father disappear? Who killed Sam?"

"I didn't say they were innocent. We're just theorizing." He leaned back on the sofa. "But what if it wasn't them, Maya? What if it was Leo? Or Chef Lucifer? Or Mr. Nice Guy from the gallery?"

"Leo is the only one besides your uncles who has the code to the private wine cellar. He's the only one who seems even slightly connected to my dad." She paused, felt her lungs tighten. "He's also fiercely loyal to your uncles. If he killed Sam, then he probably did it for them."

"So we're back to my uncles being the culprits?" Justin frowned. "I should check out the cellar again. I should take a second look at those bottles." He stood up and reached for her hand. "Come with me."

"Right now?"

He nodded, his fingers brushing hers. "I need you

to be there. To fool Leo," he added. "To make him think we're playing a sex game."

Her heart struck her chest. "We're going to mess around? On camera? Don't ask me to do that, Justin."

"We're just going to stand in front of the bottles with me bumping my fly against your butt and saying a few naughty things. I can kiss your neck, too. Nibble or whatever."

"But you're actually going to be concentrating on the bottles?"

"Yep. No naked stuff, I promise."

"Are you going to carry a portable audio jammer with you?"

He shook his head. "If the cellar is miked, I think it would be better if Leo hears what we're saying. I already threatened to give him a show, and that's what we'll be doing."

She agreed, but only because they were going to fake it. She would never do something like this for real.

They proceeded to the cellar, passing the chef and several kitchen maids along the way. When they got into the locked section, Justin set the stage.

He positioned Maya in front of the seven-bottle display and came up behind her, doing exactly what he'd told her he would do.

He slipped his arms around her waist and said, "Did you buy a see-through corset today?"

She sucked in a breath. "Yes."

"Did you try it on at the store?"

Maya nodded, and he pressed his zipper against her rear. When he nuzzled her neck, she wanted to turn around and kiss him, even with the cameras running.

So much for faking it.

"Tell me what you looked like in it," he said.

"I can put it on later. I can show you—"

He cut her off. "Tell me. I want to hear you say it."

She leaned back against him, anxious to feel the pressure of his fly. "It's white with gold trim. Strapless with boning in the front and hooks and eyelets in the back. It pushes my breasts up."

"Like this?" He moved his hands, resting them under her bosom. "Or like this?" He lifted her, even though she was already wearing an underwire bra.

"Yes, like that."

"Were your nipples poking out when you were in the store?"

"No." But they were now. Could he feel them through her bra, through her blouse?

"Did you buy anything else?"

"Yes, but—"

"But what?" he rasped against her ear.

She covered his hands with hers, pressing his palms down, wanting him to abrade her breasts. "You'll have to wait and see how sexy it is."

He rubbed her nipples through layers of fabric, making them peak even more. "Tease."

She couldn't help it. She made a dreamier sound. "You, too."

"Oh, yeah?" He spun her around and pushed her against an empty wall, his gaze locked directly on hers.

Maya knew he couldn't concentrate on the bottles anymore. By now, he was too turned on, too hungry for her. He wasn't faking it, either. He ground his hips to hers, his jeans creating hot, hard friction.

She glanced down. Bad. Bold. Mistresslike. "Can I touch you?"

He glanced down, too. "There?"

Empowered, she reached out to untuck his shirt, to skim her fingers along the waistband of his jeans. "One touch."

His eyes turned glassy; his breathing went labored. "You're going to get me naked?" he asked, reminding her that they weren't supposed to go that far.

She grazed his fly. "I'm just going to put my hand down your pants."

He groaned, but he caught her wrist. As aroused as he was, he didn't let her do it, not while they were being filmed, not while he was ready to explode.

They went back to their suite instead.

Where another game began.

Chapter 9

"Put it on," Justin said, as every nerve ending in his body screamed for relief.

"The corset?" Maya asked.

Was she being coy? "The sexy thing you wouldn't tell me about." He should be undressing her, not telling her to change into something else. But she'd piqued his hunger, his curiosity. "I want to see it."

She went to the closet and removed a garment bag, then took it into the bathroom and closed the door.

Justin unzipped his pants, just to ease the tension, the tightness, the bulge she'd offered to touch.

On camera.

He hadn't expected her to be so daring. Their affair was going at warp speed. He could only pray that they didn't crash and burn. Set each other on fire. Crumble into sexually incinerated ashes.

She came out of the bathroom, and he lost what was left of his breath.

Maya the man-eating maid.

The black plastic minidress was trimmed in white ruffles with a flounced apron. The bodice was so low, so revealing, her breasts threatened to spill out. The thigh-high hose, garter belt and hot-as-sin heels were a tantalizing touch. But when she turned around, his pulse pounded beneath his open fly.

The dress was slit way up the back, exposing ruffled panties.

"Take those off," he said.

She turned to face him. "Take what off? My fishnets? My shoes?"

"The panties, damn it. Get rid of them."

"If that's what you want." She slid them down her hips and flung them at him. The good girl had gone bad, taunting him like Stripperella.

He caught the panties in midair and shoved them in his back pocket, keeping them like a trophy. "Turn around again."

She did his bidding, bending over a little, flashing her bare bottom.

Justin couldn't help but grin. "Now that's how a maid should look."

She glanced over her shoulder. "This is the uniform I should have been wearing when you first saw me in Mr. B.'s office?"

"Hell, yes." He walked over to her, spun her back around and kissed her, open mouthed and carnal.

She tasted hot and sexy, like everything he wanted, like everything he needed.

Her panties were burning a hole in his pocket.

He deepened the kiss and reached under her dress, putting his hand between her legs. She moaned, and he used two digits, making her wet.

"You're cheating." She broke the lip lock, surfacing for air, her chest rising and falling, her eye-popping cleavage even more noticeable. "I'm supposed to be doing that to you."

"So do it." He took her hand and pushed it down the front of his jeans. He was more than ready to get felt up, to be the object of her bad-girl desire.

She closed her fingers around him, and Justin all but shivered. He felt like a fifteen-year-old virgin, desperate to lose his cherry.

"You better have protection on you." The nightstand where he kept the condoms was only a few feet away, but he didn't want to break the connection.

"I do. It's in my bra."

The contraption shoving her breasts to her chin, he thought. "Get it."

"Not yet." With only the slightest warning, she dropped to her knees and tugged down his jeans, capturing him with her mouth.

Sweet surrender.

Justin tangled his hands in her hair, and she moved in a rhythm that drove him half mad.

As the pressure built, as he lost his sanity, he pulled Maya to her feet, fished the condom out of her bra, used it and jammed her against the wall.

He wanted her like this, dark and sultry, ready to be ravished. She met his carnivorous gaze, and he hiked up her dress and plunged deep.

They mated like animals, kissing and clawing and biting. She wrapped her legs around him, and he cupped her rear, planting his hands on her cheeks and lifting her up and down for his thrusts.

If they were going to catch fire, then they would do it together.

Now. This very instant.

Damn, Maya thought. *Damn.* There was more to afterglow than cuddling. When their lovemaking ended, her heart flashed before her eyes.

After they separated, Justin went into the bathroom to get rid of the condom, and she changed her clothes, slipping into silk loungewear, trying to look less affected by what they'd just done.

She knew it was a crazy notion, but she could actually imagine spending eternity with him.

Was Tori right? Was Maya falling in love?

Justin returned, and she checked him out. His jeans were zipped, but he still had a slight ridge beneath his fly. Even with her mixed-up emotions, she smiled.

"That was the wildest sex I've ever had," she said.

He smiled, too. "Wanna do it again?"

They looked at each other and laughed. Justin never stayed sated. He always wanted more. She longed to throw her arms around him and never let go. But she didn't. She asked for her panties back instead, intending to tuck them away with the naughty maid couture.

"No way," he told her, pushing the ruffled undies farther into his pocket. "These are mine."

"Really? Well, I've got news for you, Mr. Halloway. You're going to look silly in them."

His smile disappeared. Just like that. It was gone. "My last name is Elk."

The blunder hit her like a wall of broken bricks. She moved closer, reaching out to touch the side of his face. "I know. I'm sorry. I was just—"

"Brian called me Justin Halloway when he told me about my paternity." He covered her hand with his. "I didn't expect you to say it, too. But maybe we're both losing our identities."

Or maybe it was Freudian. Maybe it was her fear of falling in love with a Hollywood Mob heir.

"Did you sign the papers?" she asked.

He stepped back, disconnecting their hands. "So I can own a portion of the mansion? Yes, I did."

"It's strange, isn't it? Your grandfather giving you so much control? I'll bet his attorney advised him against it."

He sat on the edge of the bed. "Because adding my name to the deed could create legal consequences?"

She nodded. "You could take out a loan on the property or try to force your family to sell it. You could invoke your newly acquired rights."

"That's why I signed the papers. So my uncles can't change their minds about having me as a house-guest and kick me out. So I can stay as long as I want and search for whatever happened to Sam." He snared her gaze. "And you can stay here with me."

"I appreciate that." More than he could know, more than she could tell him. She even envisioned being with him forever.

But not at the mansion.

They could get their own place in L.A. Or they could go to Texas, back to Justin's hometown. She wouldn't mind living on a recreational ranch. It seemed like a good place to settle down and raise—

"I blew it in the wine cellar," he said, jarring her

into reality. "We're going have to go back there again. But not to mess around. That's too distracting."

"Then what?"

"I don't know. But either way, Leo will be watching."

Her nerves fluttered beneath her skin, like butterflies trapped in a net. "He makes me nervous."

He stood up and came toward her, getting close once again. "I won't let anything happen to you. I swear, I won't."

He'd already let something happen to her, she thought. She'd already fallen for him. "Do you think your grandfather is part of this? That someone like Leo is reporting back to him?"

"I wondered about that, but now I'm not so sure. If good old Grandpa didn't trust me, I don't think he would have given me part of his real estate holdings."

"So he's just biding his time in maximum security without a clue?"

"In regard to Sam. It's possible. But either way, I'm starting to think that it's important for me to meet him."

"So you can try to figure him out?"

He nodded. "The best I can."

Melrose Mania, the West L.A. gallery the Halloways owned, was stark and chic, the way trendy establishments often were. Not that Justin didn't appreciate art. But this was Hutch Fielding's turf, and Justin didn't like him.

Because Maya still did. She wasn't supposed to, but he could tell that she was comfortable around Hutch. They were deep in conversation in the back room, surrounded by her paintings, laying the groundwork for her upcoming show.

Was Justin envious of Hutch? Jealous that the other man gave Maya a fatherly sense of comfort?

He glanced in their direction. Yeah, he thought. He was. But it was more than that. Something about Hutch just didn't ring true. Only *exactly* what that something was, he didn't know.

Finally Justin walked over to them. Maya and Hutch were studying one of her paintings, a female *calaca* dressed in an aristocratic manner, with a red-feathered hat seated on her bony head.

"Every day is a dance with death," Hutch said.

"Is it?" Justin asked.

Hutch kept looking at the painting. "So they say."

Justin studied the other man's profile. His manner was professional, his appearance well groomed. He wore a classic linen shirt, tan trousers and a crocodile belt. His graying-at-the-temples hair made him look like an aging fashion model, the kind you'd see in a Tommy Bahama ad.

Hutch finally turned away from the watercolor. "I

could use a break. How about some coffee? I can run over to Starbucks."

"Sure," Justin responded quickly, eager to get rid of him, even if it was only for a short while. Hutch could've asked his assistant to make the coffee run, but Justin suspected that the other man was trying to prove how unpretentious he was. Yeah, right. The Bahama guy.

"I'll take a latte," Justin told him.

"A white mocha sounds good to me," Maya said.

"Got it." Hutch smiled. "I'll be back in a flash."

Take your time, Justin thought, as the gallery manager left.

"I'm trying not to like him," Maya said.

"You're not trying very hard." Justin leaned in to kiss her, to brand her with his lips. "But at least he seems genuinely respectful of your work."

"We're putting together a phenomenal show." She made a face. "But none of this would have happened if I wasn't with you."

"Don't feel guilty that my family is promoting you. It would've raised suspicions if you'd refused their offer." He glanced at the fancy *calaca*. "She looks smug."

"She is. Rich and spoiled." Maya nudged him. "Like you."

"Oh, yeah?" He nudged her right back. He couldn't

deny her barb. Justin had become an instant billionaire. "When are you going to paint that picture for me?"

"Of the little angel? Whenever you want." She searched his gaze. "Do you think he was baptized? Do you think Reed or Beverly or Heather would have done that for him?"

"He was stillborn. They wouldn't have had the chance. *Los niños limbos,*" he added. "Children in limbo. Does it matter?"

"No. His soul would be commemorated either way."

"That's good."

"I didn't mean to make you worry about him."

"I'm not." Uncomfortable, he blew out a breath. He wished the dead baby didn't matter. He wished he didn't feel connected to it.

"Have you been in touch with your parents?" she asked.

"I've called a few times. Just to let them know I'm okay. They don't like me being here."

"In California? With the Hollywood Mob? Can you blame them?"

"No. I suppose not."

Silence stretched between them until she asked, "Where did you learn to speak Spanish, Justin?"

"From Maria." His mind drifted back to his youth. "She was the Mexican receptionist at Elk Ridge Lodge when I was growing up. She used to make the sign of the cross whenever she heard the sound of an ambulance." He smiled. "Even on TV."

Maya smiled, too. "Did she teach you about Day of the Dead? Is that how you have some knowledge of it?"

He nodded. "She made an altar for Lloyd when he died. He was the man she loved. But they never really stayed together. He had emotional problems. Post-traumatic stress or something. People sometimes thought he was crazy."

"That's sad."

"Yeah, it was. He was a gruff old cowboy, but I liked him."

"What did you think of Maria's *ofrenda?*"

"The altar? I thought it was cool. So did my sister. We wanted to eat the little candied skulls, but Maria said we weren't supposed to."

"Is Maria still around?"

"No. She died a few years ago. But I always think of her when I go to Mexico. That's where I was headed when the Halloways kidnapped me."

"To drink tequila on the beach?"

"And meet a pretty girl." He skimmed her cheek. "But I did that anyway, didn't I? I got my *señorita.*"

"Yes, you did."

He kissed her, softly, slowly, but his heart picked up speed. He cursed his reaction, but he couldn't stop it if he tried. Maya dazzled him.

He deepened the kiss, and a throat-clearing sound

caught their attention. They separated and turned to acknowledge the person who'd interrupted them.

Hutch had returned with the coffee. But he wasn't alone. Leo stood by his side.

The gallery manager handed Justin and Maya their cups. "Look who happened by," he said.

"Yeah, look who's here." Justin stared at Leo, and the Hulk stared back at him.

Hutch broke the tension, addressing Maya and Justin. "Leo and I have some business to tend to, but it shouldn't take long." He led the other man away.

Maya made a curious expression. "What do you think is going on? When I first met Hutch, he told me that Leo consults on security issues at the gallery from time to time, but this doesn't seem like a scheduled meeting. It seems more like Leo showed up out of the blue."

"Yeah, it does." Justin watched Hutch and Leo disappear into the manager's office. The Hulk seemed edgy. Justin couldn't hear the door closing from this distance, but he suspected that it had been shut with a tight click. "We can try to find out what's going on. Are you up for eavesdropping?"

"What about all of the cameras in this place?"

"We won't be seen." Security was tight to protect the art, but there weren't any lenses aimed at the manager's door.

First, he and Maya wandered over to the reception

area near Hutch's office and made sure none of the gallery employees were nearby.

"What if someone comes around the corner and catches us at his door?" she asked.

"Then we'll knock on it."

She frowned. "And say what?"

"That we're sorry for the intrusion, but we're going to order some lunch and wondered if Hutch wanted anything."

She made a face. "How thoughtful of us."

"Can you think of a better excuse? You, the woman who hid in a utility room to spy on the mob?"

"You're right. Let's do this."

They got closer to where they needed to be, walking as soundlessly as possible.

Someone was shuffling back and forth, moving inside the office. Restless steps. Leo, Justin thought. Sometimes he was heavy-footed, his fancy Italian loafers rebelling to support his weight. Hutch was probably seated behind his desk. He seemed like the type to kick back while Leo paced.

Justin strained to hear the conversation. Maya did, too. Words were exchanged, but nothing was clear. Then the men's voices raised a decibel, enough to filter through the hollow door.

Leo seemed concerned about their next "job," and the gallery manager told the security chief to relax, that he had everything under control.

The pacing stopped.

Justin and Maya held their breaths.

Leo questioned Hutch about a dollar amount. A six-figure number was bandied about. A few seconds later, Leo referred to their "buyer," asking if Hutch was sure, "absolutely sure" the buyer could be trusted since they'd never sold anything to him before.

When Mr. Cool behind the desk insisted that he knew his business, that his art connections were sound, Justin glanced at Maya, and she widened her eyes.

The scenario seemed obvious. Leo and Hutch were dealing in stolen art, selling pieces to private collectors who knew what they were buying had been ripped off.

Leo's footsteps sounded again, only louder this time, drowning out the rest of their conversation.

Shit.

The security chief was moving away from the vicinity of Hutch's desk and walking toward the door. There was no time to escape, to get out of the line of fire.

The doorknob turned.

Justin reacted, lifting his hand to knock. The door swung open, and he practically rapped on Leo's chest.

"Oops. Sorry." Justin barked out a sarcastic laugh. "Weird timing. Maya and I are ordering lunch. We figured Hutch might be hungry."

"Really?" The Hulk stared him down, the ever-present tension between them palpable. "What about me?"

Maya sidestepped the situation, and Justin did what he always did. He held the other man's hard stare. "We didn't think you'd be hanging around long enough to eat."

"Sounds like you're trying to get rid of me."

"Maybe we are," Justin responded, without moving out of the way. He purposely blocked Leo in the open doorway.

Seconds ticked by.

Justin finally moved. He could tell that Leo suspected them of eavesdropping, but it was too late to do anything about it now. The Hulk bumped Justin's shoulder as he passed.

After the security chief left the gallery, Hutch approached Maya and Justin with a don't-mind-Leo smile.

"Lunch sounds great," he told them, behaving as if nothing out of the ordinary had just happened.

Later that day, Maya and Justin took Lester to the garden. It was Lester's favorite place at the mansion. He loved to romp the grassy grounds and stick his nose in scented buds. The dog was in flower-power heaven.

But Maya wasn't.

She looked at Justin. He stood beside a freestanding trellis. Lacy leaves climbed the gothic structure,

twining around decorative steel, giving her a conflict-
ing chill.

"I wish we hadn't gotten caught at the door," she
said.

"They can't be sure of how much we overheard.
If we overheard anything at all."

"I should have listened to you about Hutch. I
should have known better."

"It isn't your fault that he reminds you of your
dad. That he—"

"That he what?" she prodded. Justin's expression
had turned much too tight.

"What if his mannerisms are deliberate? What if
he's been behaving like Sam on purpose? What if
Leo figured out who you are, and he told Hutch to
play mind games with you?"

Her heart punched her chest, and the chill got colder,
more pronounced. She knew it was possible, but she
didn't want to face it, to think too deeply about it. "It
could be a coincidence that he reminds me of my dad."

"A creepy coincidence," her lover said.

Maya rubbed the goose bumps on her arms. Now
the lacy leaves climbing along the trellis reminded her
of the human-eating plants in *Little Shop of Horrors*.

Justin moved closer and reached for her hand,
holding it protectively in his. "I meant what I said
about keeping you safe."

"From Hutch? From Leo? From your own family?" She tugged her hand away from his. "I wish you weren't related to the mob. I wish you were a normal guy, someone I met in an average situation."

He frowned. "You weren't supposed to regret being with me."

Suddenly Maya's world crashed in on her. Sleeping with Justin wasn't a sin. But loving him? Wanting to marry him? Have his babies?

Little Halloway heirs.

"I didn't bargain for this," she said. "It scares me."

"What does? Having a future with me? We never made any promises to each other."

"No, we didn't." But her mind kept straying in that direction. "Sometimes girls go off on romantic tangents."

"We'll just keep it physical, okay?" He tried to reassure her. "We'll just do the man-mistress thing."

Like Tori and Brian, she thought. And David and Nancy. That scared her, too. But she agreed in spite of herself. "The sex *is* good."

"It's better than good."

He took her in his arms, and Maya clung to him, her fingers fisting his shirt. Why did being physical with him have to be so damn emotional? Why couldn't she keep her heart out of it?

"Sometimes guys get romantic notions, too." He ended the hug. "We're the ones who buy diamond rings, who get on bended knees and propose."

Her chest turned tight. "Is that what you did with Claire before you walked away?"

He defended himself. "I already told you that she was better off without me."

The dog ran past them with a daisy in his mouth, but they ignored the puppy's antics.

"What do we do now?" she asked.

In spite of the tension between them, Justin didn't miss a beat. He picked up on her thoughts, on the abrupt change of topic. "About solving your father's case? We'll keep trying. We'll keep investigating until we get some evidence to take to the authorities. Telling them what we overheard today would never be enough. We don't even know if it has anything to do with Sam."

"No, we don't."

"Maybe we should focus on the wine cellar again," Justin said. "We could have dinner in there tonight."

"To check out the bottles one more time?"

"To check everything out. Sam disappeared while the place was under construction. We haven't investigated that angle."

"So you're going examine the way it was built? Over dinner?"

"Why not? There's a table in there. We can ask the chef to pack us a nighttime picnic."

"Leo is going to watch us."

"What can he say? I'll be subtle about looking

around. Mostly I'll be having an intimate meal with you." He paused, searched her gaze, his eyes locking deliberately onto hers. "Unless this is problem for you. Unless faking a romantic situation with me is more than you can deal with right now."

"As long as you protect our conversation this time. I don't want to have to be conscious of everything I say." Or to lose focus, she thought. And get romantic for real.

"I'll bring the portable audio jammer. I'll put it in my pocket."

"Then there's no problem. I can handle it." Needing a diversion, she glanced away and caught sight of Lester. The daisy was gone, and the dog had dirt all over his face, a telltale sign that he'd buried the delicate posy. "I can handle it just fine."

Chapter 10

Maya set the table with silver, chinaware and crisp linens, all of which had come from the elegant basket the chef had provided.

The meal consisted of eggplant appetizer, walnut spinach salad, smoked chicken and cold pasta. For dessert, they'd be eating flan.

Wine, of course, was a must. Justin cracked open a bottle of Riesling, chosen to complement the main course, a suggestion many wineries made as well. He poured it into handcrafted, twenty-four-percent lead crystal glasses. Maya knew, because the Halloways only used the best.

She took a sip, tasting stone fruits: peach, pear and apricot.

"Do you like it?" he asked.

She nodded and drank a bit more. She needed the buzz.

In the background, a CD collection of country ballads swept the air. Justin had set up a portable stereo, adding extra ambience.

"I've been making nonstop love to you, and you're still a mystery to me," he said.

Maya filled their plates. She'd asked him to protect their conversation so they could speak freely. And this was what he wanted to talk about? This was his way of faking a romantic dinner? Putting her in the hot seat? Then again, they were being filmed. They had to look as if they were engrossed in each other.

"Tell me how you old are," he said next. "I don't even know your birthday."

"I'm twenty-six, and I was born on March tenth."

"That would make you a Pisces. Sensitive, secretive." He smiled. "Artistic and dreamy, too. It fits."

She added more chicken to his plate and handed it to him, trying to keep her Piscean tendencies under control. His smile never failed to make her weak. "This is so seventies."

"What is? Talking about astrology?"

"Yes." She went after her wine again.

"Then we'll talk about something else." He gave a slight pause. "Have you ever lived with anyone?"

"No." She was living with him, sharing his suite, his bed, but she decided not to point that out. "I dated a musician for three years. We talked about getting a place together, but we never did."

"What was his name?"

"Todd." Tall and lanky, she thought, with shaggy hair and urban tattoos. "He was in an alternative rock band."

"Why didn't your relationship last?"

"Our creative differences got in the way. Two artists butting heads."

Justin stood up and walked over the wine display, taking his Riesling with him. He leaned against the edge of the wood and took in his surroundings, probably making mental notes in his head, memorizing every nook and cranny.

Maya relaxed, grateful the cellar had consumed him. He moved to the other side of the room, where empty pegs dominated an entire wall, where there was no wine, no displays.

"What do you think?" she asked.

"About what?"

"This place?"

He traced an empty peg, following the shape with his fingers. "It looks okay to me. But I'm not an architect. I could be missing something. I could be missing lots of things."

He gazed up at the ceiling, then shifted his attention back to her, to the conversation they'd had earlier. Zoom. Zap. She couldn't escape.

"Were you in love with Todd?" he asked.

She shook her head. "It wasn't that intense."

"So you've never been in love?"

She glanced at her food. She couldn't bear to look at him and lie. But she wasn't about to admit how she felt about him, either. "No."

"I proposed to Claire like this. At an intimate dinner," he clarified. "I popped the question during dessert."

She gave up the fight and looked at him. "Why are you telling me this?"

"Because I want you to know that I didn't mean to hurt her. I ended the engagement because the closer we got to the wedding date, the more I panicked."

"About losing your freedom?"

"About marrying the wrong girl. I loved Claire, but I realized that I wasn't *in* love with her. There's a difference."

"I know. There are all kinds of love. Mom and I talked about that before she died."

"When she admitted how she felt about your father?"

Maya nodded. "And how he *didn't* feel about her."

"My parents, the ones who raised me, have always been in love. Even when they weren't together." Justin frowned. "So were Reed and Beverly.

Or that's what I've been told. Who the hell knows about Reed?"

"I never came across a picture of him when I was researching the Halloways."

"My mom has old photos of him around."

She finished her Riesling. "Was he handsome when he was young? Was he dark and wild-looking?"

He returned to the table. "I guess, yeah."

"Like you," she said.

Justin's frown deepened. "I suppose there's a resemblance. But nothing uncanny. Nothing that gave away my paternity."

Time slipped by and their conversation faded. They ate in silence, but when they finished the main course, neither of them touched the flan.

She wasn't sure why. Maybe because he'd proposed to another woman over dessert.

"Do you want to dance?" he asked, as Tim McGraw sang about stars going blue.

"So we can spend more time here? So you can look around some more?"

He nodded, and as he reached for her hand, a Hank Williams, Sr. tune came on.

"Wedding Bells."

Bad timing, she thought. But she moved into his arms, and he led her in a gentle two-step, their feet gliding just above the floor.

"You're a good dancer," he said.

"I took lessons when I was a teenager. Mom thought it would help me get dates. You should see me salsa."

"Oh, yeah." He nudged her hips against his, and for a heart-blasting moment, the two-step got dirty.

Sweet Lord. "You're good, too."

He laughed, then went back to the beat. "I learned at the ranch. We have dances every week. Mostly country. But sometimes they play other music, too."

"Sounds like a fun place."

"It is. It was. But that didn't stop me from getting bored. Living in a small town can get monotonous. I guess Reed felt that way, too. God, I hate him."

She started. She shouldn't have been shocked by his harsh words. But she hadn't expected to hear them in the middle of a dance, in the midst of being in his arms. "I think he did the right thing, giving you to Michael and Heather, protecting you from the Halloways."

"Yeah, and look where it got me."

She went achy inside. "Mixed up with me?"

"I didn't mean it like that, Maya."

"I know." But it was true for both of them. They woke up every day, caught in the danger that had brought them together. "Maybe we should finish our meal."

She went back to the table and picked up her spoon. She shouldn't give up dessert just because he'd proposed to Claire over something sweet.

He stood off to the side, watching her.

"Wedding Bells" ended, making way for another tragic love song. "Are you going to eat?" she asked.

He sat down and tasted the flan. "You're still a mystery to me."

"Like this cellar?" she asked.

"I hope not." He studied the architecture again, and they barely spoke, barely looked at each other, discomfort steeping between them.

At bedtime Justin and Maya lay side by side. The sheers on the windows were open, showcasing midnight mergers, blurring the moon and stars. On the nightstand closest to Justin, a Tiffany lamp burned low, sending stained-glass shadows across the sheets.

Muted ambience.

He turned to look at Maya. She wore a shimmering nightgown with threads of silver running through it. The fabric was light and soft with a rainlike quality.

"Can I touch you?" he asked.

She angled her head toward his. Her hair, long and loose, bunched against a satin-draped pillow. "You don't have to ask permission."

"Tonight I feel like I do."

Emotions ran rampant, and he wasn't sure what to do about it. Aside from possessing her, he thought. From taking what she was willing to give.

He glided his hand along her neck and over her shoulders. Her skin was smooth and slightly scented.

Maya rarely wore fragrances, and when she did, the effect seemed misty.

Like her nightgown.

She wasn't naked underneath. Her breasts were bare, but she had panties on.

He leaned on top of her, intent on kissing her, on pressing his body to hers. He wasn't naked, either. He wore cotton boxers.

She wrapped her arms around him, and he welcomed the sensation. Their lips met in a heart-stirring way, and he slipped the front of her nightgown down.

Maya arched and sighed.

He lowered his head and took one of her nipples in his mouth, making it pucker beneath his tongue.

"I should pour caramel all over you," he said.

She watched him. "Like the flan?"

"Mexican custard. A Mexican girl." He moved to her other nipple. "Sweet heaven. You taste good."

She watched him suckle. "Can you cook?"

"Not very well." He left wetness on her skin. "But I'm sure I could melt caramel in a pot."

"Mmm." She made a yummy sound. "What kind of treat can I turn you into?"

He smiled against her breast. "How about Cherokee bread pudding? It has maple syrup in it."

"That works for me." She lifted his hair off of his forehead. "My Justin."

"My, my, my Maya."

He removed her nightgown and dropped it onto the floor. Her panties came next. She opened her thighs and he put his mouth there, pleasuring her as intimately as he could.

He cupped her bottom, and she lifted her hips. He knew she liked what he was doing. He knew it was the foreplay that drove her to the brink of sexual destruction.

Only tonight, it seemed like more than eroticism, more than a warm, wet game. More than dessert, he thought. Than custard or caramel or anything else he could imagine.

"Make it happen when you're inside me," she said.

He refused her request. "I want to make it happen now *and* when I'm inside you."

He used his mouth on her until she shivered and shuddered all over him.

Justin loved every second of it.

Satisfied that he'd made them both hot, he grabbed a condom from the nightstand and handed it to her. She tore open the package and sheathed him. A rubber had never felt so good.

"What am I going to do with you?" she asked.

"You're already doing it."

He entered her, getting as close as humanly possible. He chose the missionary position so he could look into her eyes. But he wanted to kneel behind her, too.

They made love both ways, and the penetration was deep and strong, their bodies tightly joined. For now, all that mattered was being with Maya.

She kissed him until he moaned, and he gave her another orgasm and followed her into the storm.

Maya awakened in a fog and reached for Justin, but his side of the bed was empty. She sat up, squinted in the dark and noticed a light under the door.

He was in the living room? She glanced at the clock. At three-thirty-two in the morning?

She put on her robe and followed the light.

He sat on the sofa, deep in thought, gazing at a spiral notebook in his hand. His hair was mussed and he wore a pair of boxer shorts, his usual sleeping attire. Only she suspected that he hadn't slept a wink. There was a soda can, a pencil and a ruler on the table beside him.

"What's going on?" she asked, getting his attention.

He glanced up. "I think I figured it out."

She moved closer, nervous, excited, curious. "Tell me."

"It's going to sound strange."

"Tell me," she repeated, and sat next to him. They didn't have to worry about being overheard. She knew the audio jammers were still in place. Justin checked them daily.

"Your dad's design isn't right. I've never done an architectural drawing before, but since I have some basic construction knowledge and I'm good at mathematical equations, I decided to give it a try." He frowned at the notebook. "And it doesn't mesh."

She forced herself to breathe. "Why? What's wrong with the way it was designed?"

"First of all, there's a glue-laminated beam, a glulam, supporting the ceiling above the wall with the empty wine rack. Glulams are used as extra reinforcement, like in oversized garage openings." He lifted the notebook. "It didn't hit me until I started working on the drawing. Until I put it on paper."

She glanced at his sketch and saw how precise it was. "What else doesn't mesh?"

"The temperature of the room seems correct and all that, but there isn't adequate space above or behind the empty rack for the hot air exhaust from the cooling system to dissipate properly. The dimensions are off. So are the dimensions above and behind the seven-bottle rack."

"It's not a wine cellar at all."

"Nope. It looks like one, it feels like one, but it isn't."

Her mind reeled, and she wondered what her father had gotten himself into.

"I think the wall with the empty rack is a door of some kind," he said. "That it opens, along with the wall it's attached to."

"That's why the ceiling is reinforced?"

He nodded. "And the seven bottles are the electronic key that opens the door. Obviously they aren't real wine. They're dummies. Bottles made to look like real vintages with colored water or something inside of them."

Her pulse pounded in her ears. "So they really are *the key* to all this?"

"Yes." He set down the notebook and reached for his soda, taking a long hard swallow. "And this is how I think the key works. The sequence of the bottles has to be changed, and once they're placed in the appropriate pegs, the door opens."

"So what's the order of the bottles?"

"That's the part I haven't figured out. And we can't just go down and start moving them around, hoping we'll stumble upon the right sequence."

She wracked her brain, desperate to help. "Maybe the bottles are coded. Maybe the labels are a clue."

"That's what I've been thinking. But how do we break the code? How do we unravel it?" He finished his drink. "Is it alphabetical? Numerical? Is it related to the winery? To the grape variety?"

Maya moved to the edge of the sofa, her heart dangling, her emotions hanging by a breakable thread. "Do you think what we overheard is related to this? Do you think they're storing stolen art behind that secret door?"

He made a troubled face. "It seems possible. And if they are, they're probably smuggling it in empty barrels or wooden crates, carting it down there like wine."

Her heart dangled even farther. "Does that mean that my dad was a criminal, too? That his dirty dealings got him killed?"

He gave her an honest answer. "I don't know. I'm hoping there's another explanation, something that puts him in a better light. But at the moment, he seems as guilty as the rest of them."

She blinked back the tears gathering in her eyes. "He was so proud that I was an artist. He respected what I did. I can't imagine him desecrating the art world."

"Then we'll think good thoughts about him until we know for sure."

They sat quietly until she asked, "If we do break the code, how are we going to use it?"

"Without getting caught on camera? I haven't gotten that far yet. I've got a lot of details to consider." He studied her. "Maybe we should go to the FBI. Maybe we should share our suspicions with them."

"Don't you think we should wait until we have something concrete? Until we break the code and see what's down there?"

He traced the angle of her jaw. "If we tell the FBI who you are, maybe they can protect you."

Her heart tagged after his. "I'd feel safer being with you."

"Are you sure?"

"Yes," she responded. He'd already promised that he wouldn't let anything happen to her, and she believed him.

"Then I'll work that much harder to solve this case, to keep my family from hurting you."

He stood up and walked over to the gas fireplace, flipped the switch and turned on the flame. Silent, he ripped his drawing from the notebook and burned it, keeping it out of the wrong hands.

Maya stood up, too. "Let's go back to bed."

He turned away from the fire, facing her once again. "I won't be able to sleep."

"Me neither." But she wanted to stay awake in his arms. Even if being in love with him still scared her, even if it was a danger he couldn't promise to protect her from.

Chapter 11

Time passed quickly with Justin's mind working overtime. He was still immersed in the code, hoping he would stumble upon something that made sense, something that was significant to his family. Whatever the sequence was, he hoped there was a rhyme or a reason behind it. If not, he was screwed. How would he recognize a random code?

As for Maya, her art show was fast approaching. Between the two of them, their heads were spinning.

But even more so today. Justin was scheduled to visit his grandfather this afternoon. His paperwork had been approved.

"Are you going alone?" Maya asked. "Or are your uncles going with you?" She stood in their cozy kitchen, cleaning up their breakfast dishes. She'd cooked for him earlier.

"I'm going by myself. My grandfather doesn't want anyone else there." He moved forward, desperate to kiss her, to hold her close. "I hate leaving you alone."

"I'll be fine. I'll be in my studio, working on your painting." She touched his jaw. "Thinking about you."

He looked into her eyes, and his heart did an uneasy flop. Romantic confusion. The most dangerous of liaisons.

He stepped back, and she dropped her hand.

"What's wrong?"

"Nothing." Was he fooling himself into believing that he could let her go when all of this was over? That he could walk away? Return to his old life? Survive without her? "I'm just stressing about seeing my grandfather."

"I don't blame you."

"I'm going to bring up the wine cellar if I can. Since he supposedly had reservations about it."

"That's a good idea. You can gauge his response."

"Yeah." He leaned forward to kiss her again, to take one more taste, one more possessive connection.

Hell and damnation.

Before he could admit that he was falling in love, he did his rugged best to escape with his heart in a steady condition. The uneasy flops were new to him. He'd never gotten that way over Claire, and he'd been astute enough to know that he should've.

"I better take off," he said, clawing a hand through his hair. "It's a long drive."

Maya wished him luck with his grandfather, and they went their separate ways. She locked herself in her studio, and Justin stood outside of her door and cursed his scattered emotions. She'd already told him that having a future with him scared her. They'd already agreed that they weren't headed in that direction.

Yet here he was, panicked about losing her, doing a lousy job of sticking to his end of the bargain.

Determined to focus on his trip, he left the mansion and took his Porsche to the prison, a facility located about two hours north of L.A.

Once he got there, he followed procedure, passing through a metal detector, presenting his ID and signing a visitor's log.

He was told that handshakes, hugs and kisses—in good taste—were permitted at the beginning and end of each visit. He'd been hoping to see his grandfather behind a glass enclosure with telephones for communication. But that wasn't the case. Denny had general population privileges.

The visiting room consisted of dull gray walls and circular tables with plastic seats bolted to the floor. Various vending machines were available, but inmates were restricted from handling money. If Denny wanted a snack, Justin would have to get it for him.

The place was packed with families and a lot of them were drinking sodas and eating chips and sandwiches. Kids nibbled on candy.

When Justin came face to face with his grandfather, he took a deep breath. Denny wore starched prison blues and an awed expression. The older man reached out to hug him. The embrace was quick and awkward.

They sat across from each other. Denny looked every bit his age. At eighty-seven, the lines on his face grooved deeply into his skin, and his hair thinned into wisps of gray.

"I saw you when you were little," Denny said. "You probably even had that toy with you. I looked right at you, but I didn't know you belonged to Beverly. I didn't know you were her boy."

Justin shifted in his chair. Richard had warned him that his grandpa might cry, and the tears seemed genuine. He had to remind himself that Denny had been incarcerated for conspiracy to commit murder.

"Where was I? When did this happen?"

"Heather and Michael brought you to the mansion a few days before Beverly died. She'd asked to see them, to say goodbye. But now I know it was you she wanted to see. You she was saying goodbye to." His voice choked up. "Her son."

Justin steeled his emotions. "I'm Reed's kid, too. Everyone keeps telling me that I'm like him."

"Your dad was smart and savvy. Bold, brash, young, arrogant. Everything the West Coast Family was looking for." Denny stalled for a moment. "If he'd been loyal to our organization, I would have given him my blessing to marry your mother. I would have loved him like a son."

"But he betrayed you?"

"He was supposed to assist in a hit. But at the last minute, he purposely screwed up, trying to stop it."

For once Justin had to give Reed credit for doing the right thing, for not wanting to be part of a murder. "Was he successful? Did he stop it?"

"No. The hit went down anyway, and Reed was there when it happened. He was an accessory." Denny sighed. "Later, after Beverly died, he testified against me and cut a deal with the feds."

"And that was the end of it?"

"Not necessarily." The old man leaned in close. "There's something I want to tell you, something even your uncles don't know."

Justin leaned forward, too. He couldn't help it. He wanted to hear what his grandpa had to say.

"The hit on Reed was called off a long time ago," Denny whispered. "The government didn't need to change his identity. He isn't in danger of dying."

Good God. "Is this a joke?"

"Far from it. During the time Reed was on the run with Beverly and Heather, I had fully intended to have him killed. But after Heather brought Beverly back home, everything changed." Denny's eyes turned watery again. "Beverly was riddled with cancer. My sweet, beautiful girl was dying, wasting away."

Justin saw her, frail and lost, in his mind. "I'm sorry," was all he could think to say.

His grandfather continued, "She called me to her bedside and begged me not to kill Reed. Not to murder the man she loved. Those were her last words. That was the last thing she ever said to me."

Justin's eyes went misty, too. Just enough to make him uncomfortable. He cleared his throat.

Denny continued, "I couldn't kill Reed, not without dishonoring my daughter. So I called off the hit and kept quiet about it. I wasn't about to look weak. Not to my sons, my peers, or the feds. I had a reputation to uphold."

"What about the hitman? Weren't you concerned that he'd tell someone in your organization?"

"He was freelance. He wasn't one of my people. Besides, he'd already been paid. It was no skin off his nose."

"So Reed entered WITSEC for nothing?"

"The government didn't know that he wasn't in danger. They still don't."

Justin struggled to make sense of it. "Why are you telling me all of this?"

"Because I want you to know the truth. That I spared his life." Denny was still leaning close, still keeping their conversation as private as the situation would allow. "I wish Beverly wouldn't have kept you a secret. We missed out on so much together. I love you, Justin. The way I loved her."

The walls started closing in. "You don't even know me."

"I know you through my daughter. She carried you in her womb. You're a Halloway. You're part of us. Of our legacy."

The walls got narrower, the room getting smaller. "Do you believe that Brian and Richard disbanded the mob?"

"I don't know. I honestly don't. But it doesn't matter because our family will always be associated with organized crime. That sort of notoriety never goes away." Denny paused. "Are you angry that I told your uncles to kidnap you? That I wanted you to understand who you are and where you come from?"

"I was angry at first. I'm not anymore." Justin changed the subject. "What do you think of Leo?"

The old man lifted his eyebrows. "He wasn't important during my regime. But I heard that he worked his way up the ranks. Don't you like him?"

"No. He's a bastard."

"Want me to have him killed for you?"

Justin bit back a smile. Good old Grandpa had a sense of humor. "Are you making me an offer I can't refuse?"

Denny stifled a grin, too.

A moment later they both went silent, and the noisy environment intensified: voices buzzing, food wrappers crackling, a cranky toddler whining on his mama's knee.

"Am I supposed to tell my parents that Reed can come home now?" Justin finally asked. "Am I supposed to let the government know that he isn't in danger?"

"Do you want Reed to come home?" came the wary reply. "Do you want to get to know him?"

"Truthfully? I don't want him anywhere near me. I know I'm not supposed to fault for him for trying to protect me. He entrusted me to my parents, and they gave me a loving home. I can't imagine not be longing to them...."

"But?" his grandfather prodded.

"But I feel like Reed washed his hands of me. He didn't have to sever all ties. He didn't have to ask my parents to lie to me. He could have relied on the letters and phone calls WITSEC provides. He could have told me that I was his son. Explained his side of the story." The hurt got deeper. "But he just went on with his life. He even got married."

"Really?"

"Yeah." Justin tensed. "A long time ago. WIT-SEC got word to my parents about it. It's the only time Reed ever allowed any contact to be made. For all I know, he's got other kids. Maybe even grand-kids."

"Then forget about that self-serving SOB. Forget that he's your father. But don't forget that Beverly is your mother. She didn't abandon you. She died. That isn't the same thing."

"I know. I don't blame her." Justin decided this was the time to ask Denny about the wine cellar, to weave it into the conversation. "Richard told me that you wanted them to stop completion on the cellar they built for Beverly. That you thought the architect disappearing tainted it."

"That's true. I did. I still do."

"I wasn't sure if my mother really was interested in collecting wine."

"She was. Very much so. We were going to buy a collection for her on her twenty-first birthday. But she'd run off with Reed by then." Denny gave him a perplexed look. "Why didn't you think that her interest in wine was real? Because the cellar is fake and the bottles are dummies?"

Justin's heart blasted his chest. "Yes." He hesitated, coming up with an excuse to cover his tracks. "But don't mention to my uncles that we had this conversation. I'd prefer to keep anything that has to do with my mother private. Just between us."

"That's fine with me. It turned into a bad omen. Not a good way to honor Beverly. The feds were all over Brian and Richard, accusing them of being involved in the architect's disappearance."

Another heartbeat blast. "How much does the FBI know about the cellar?"

"They know it's a vault that was designed to house your uncles' art collection. Brian showed them the blueprints, the permits, the whole shebang."

A legitimate art vault? Damn. Justin hadn't expected the secret door to be part of a permitted structure. He'd assumed that Sam had designed it to be built on the sly.

"The feds finally dropped the investigation," his grandfather said. "But having Beverly associated with it still upsets me."

"Do you know what the code is? Or what it means?"

Denny shook his head. "Your uncles were going to compile a list of the original wines we were going to give Beverly and let me pick which bottles should be used, which ones should be made into dummies. But I didn't want to do that after the architect disappeared. So they kept me out of it."

"They're keeping me out, too."

"It's just as well. I'm telling you, your mother wouldn't have liked that place. Not if she knew the man who'd designed it had gone missing."

"I'm sorry you lost her," Justin said, thinking that Beverly sounded like a sweet girl.

"She loved her family. But she hated what we represented, what we did. Do you think God punished me by taking her? Do you think losing my daughter was my penance?"

"I don't know. But I understand how she felt. I'm mixed up about being a Halloway."

"So am I," his grandfather admitted. "Sometimes I'm ashamed of my past. And other times I'm not." He blew out a tight breath. "I'm not a good role model. I'm not a good man. But I still want to be part of your life."

It was more than Reed wanted, Justin thought. More than he'd been willing to do.

And that counted for something.

When visiting hours ended, Justin and Denny were forced to say goodbye. But this time the hug didn't seem quite so awkward.

Justin and Maya were in bed, fighting the midnight hour. Neither of them could sleep. For the past four days, since Justin had seen Denny, he and Maya had been batting around ideas. Finally they'd come to the conclusion that his uncles could be smuggling stolen art into the vault with legitimate pieces. That didn't explain why Maya's father had gone missing, but it explained why the FBI investigation had gone nowhere. There was nothing illegal that tied Sam to the Halloways, at least not that the feds were aware of. As far as they knew, the vault had been built for a legitimate art collection.

"Are you okay?" Maya asked suddenly.

"I'm fine. I'm just preoccupied." He indicated the spiral notebook in his hand. Whenever he could, he immersed himself in information from the wine bottle labels, writing things down, burning them later. "I'm working on the code."

"That isn't it. You've been distant."

Because he was keeping a secret, he thought. He hadn't told Maya about Reed. He didn't want her to know that he had the power to bring his biological father home. If he told her, she would take Reed's side. She wouldn't understand why Justin couldn't bear to meet him.

Guilt pummeled his heart. His parents wouldn't understand, either. They would want Reed back in their lives.

He changed the subject. "I figured out a way to disable the security cameras in the cellar and run a tape of old footage, so it'll look like the place is empty."

She shifted to a more upright position. "You mean we can go down there and Leo won't see us on the monitor?"

He nodded. "I researched the system. It shouldn't be too difficult."

"Are you kidding? It would be difficult for most

people. You can do amazing things, Justin." She studied him from beneath her lashes. "But I shouldn't be surprised, I guess. Reed was an electronics expert."

Among other things, he thought.

"You inherited a lot from him."

"Yeah, but it doesn't matter until I crack the code." Nor did he want to dwell on all of the so-called brilliant attributes he possessed that had come from Reed, even if he couldn't deny that he had his father's technical mind.

"I'm sorry I haven't been much help." She arched her back, stretching her muscles. "My brain doesn't work like yours."

"Your brain works just fine. You're a smart girl."

"Why?" She sent him a teasing smile. "Because I'm crazy about you?"

He didn't tease her back. He couldn't, not in his lack-of-humor mood. He set the notebook aside and took her in his arms, encouraging her to lie down with him. She nuzzled his shoulder, and he stroked a hand down her hair.

Everything in his life was so damn uncertain. His family. His future. His relationship with Maya. The possibility that he loved her.

How messed up could he be?

He touched her cheek and cursed himself for not being honest, for not being able to bring her into the deepest, darkest parts of his soul.

"Will you paint a *calaca* of Beverly?" he asked instead.

"You've been thinking a lot about her lately."

"Denny made me feel closer to her. I could tell it broke his heart when she died."

"Her death probably broke Reed's heart, too."

"He wasn't even there when she died. He doesn't matter."

Maya sighed, but she didn't push the issue.

"So will you paint a *calaca* of her?" he asked again, involving Maya the only way he knew how.

"Of course I will. As soon as I'm done with the little angel." She snuggled even closer. "I'll bet Beverly is watching over him."

"Denny asked me not to forget her."

"You won't," she said before she drifted off to sleep.

Maya was right. Justin hadn't forgotten Beverly.

But not just because of what Denny had said. On the day of Maya's art show, Justin knew he'd unraveled the code.

He approached Maya while she was getting ready in the bathroom, putting on her makeup.

"There's something I need to show you," he said.

She turned toward him, eyeliner pencil in hand. The mirror reflected the back of her head and the jeweled combs in her hair.

"What is it?" she asked.

He removed a piece of paper from his pocket.

She looked at it. "I don't understand. Y-V-B-L-R-E-E? What does that mean?"

"They're the first letters from each winery. It's an anagram."

Maya squinted. "I've never been good at those."

"Here." He grabbed her eyeliner and used it to put the letters in order.

She read them and gasped. "BEVERLY. Oh, my goodness. Is that the code?"

"Denny would think it's a really bad omen. That my uncles were able to construct my mother's name from wines she had on her list. But I'm convinced this is it. If we put the bottles in the correct sequence, Beverly can open the vault."

Her voice vibrated. "When are we going to do this? When is it going to happen?"

"Tonight. At the after party." The Halloways had decided to do more than host a reception at the gallery. They'd organized a shindig for afterward, too.

She gave him an incredulous look. "The mansion will be filled with people."

"It's perfect timing. Parties are always hectic for Leo and his crew. Hopefully they'll be too busy to keep a close eye on us."

"Did you disable the cameras already? And run that tape?"

"No, but I will."

"What about your uncles? What if they notice that we're gone from the party?"

"We'll take a walk in the garden, then we'll slip around to the back of the house and enter the kitchen and wine cellar that way."

She got weak-kneed and sat on the closed lid of the commode. "I've been waiting for this, and now it seems like it's happening so fast."

"Do you want me to do it alone?" he asked.

"No. I can handle it. I just need to take a moment to breathe."

"It'll be okay. I promised to protect you, and I will. I'd die before I'd let anything happen to you."

"Don't talk like that." She stood up to put her arms around him. "Don't even think it."

He closed his eyes and held her against his heart. He couldn't help what he was saying, what he was feeling. Because tonight of all nights, he couldn't deny the truth.

That he loved her.

Chapter 12

Maya stood in the crowded ballroom, a drink in her hand. Her show had been a tremendous success and the after party was in full swing.

She had always dreamed about a night like this, where the art world would take notice of her, where she earned praise and respect, where international collectors who shaped the market had purchased her work.

But in her dreams, the Hollywood Mob hadn't been by her side. They hadn't been funding her show, promoting her because she was one of their mistresses.

She glanced at Justin. His shirt captured a spattering of neon colors, a deliberate effect from flashing lights.

The ballroom had been transformed into a south-of-the-border style disco. A DJ played a mixture of American, European and Latin tunes, spinning fast rhythmic songs.

The Halloways loved themed parties, and this was for Maya. This was her night.

Her discomfort, she thought.

And her fear.

She and Justin had been dancing and socializing, faking their way through the festivities. But soon they would slip off to the wine cellar to unlock the Beverly door.

Maya lifted the virgin margarita in her hand and took a sip. She wasn't about to consume alcohol tonight. Justin was sober, as well. He'd been drinking club sodas with twists of lime.

He stood a few feet away, talking to an ageless woman in a minidress and knee-high boots. She owned a posh London gallery, and she'd purchased a Day of the Dead painting, intrigued by "Maya's modern influence on folk art." Maya had spoken to her earlier.

Finally Justin and the guest parted ways. She dashed off to dance to Shakira and he approached Maya, whispering in her ear.

"Ready?" he asked.

She nodded and set her drink on a nearby table. A glittery purse was slung over her shoulder. She had a camera phone inside of it. Justin had one too, tucked away in his pocket. They intended to take pictures of whatever they found in the vault.

He took her arm and escorted her into the garden. Guests milled around. Some cooled themselves in the night air, and some gathered in smoke-filled hazes, taking outdoor cigarette breaks.

Justin and Maya kept walking, moving away from the party and farther into the moonlight, as if they were going on a romantic stroll.

By the time they reached the side of the mansion where a back door led to the kitchen, her heart was pounding beneath her breast. The door was locked, but that didn't stop Justin. He produced a key.

"I own part of this place," he said.

"Yes, of course." It made sense that he had a back door key. Maya just wished that she could breathe a little clearer. That the air in her lungs wasn't so choppy.

They entered the kitchen and headed directly for the cellar stairs. A wall blocked them from the chef and his staff. Lucifer didn't have a clue.

Justin didn't put the rest of their plan into action, not right away. Once they were locked in the phony cellar, he took her in his arms and pressed his lips to hers. A warm and tender kiss. Her heart pounded even faster.

"I want us to be together," he said, still holding

onto her. "No matter what happens after this. No matter how it ends."

"Wh-y?" she asked, tripping over the word. "Why are you telling me this now?"

"Because I want you to know. I need you to know."

She didn't say anything else. She couldn't find her voice. She'd already contemplated staying with him. She'd already panicked about it.

Without taking up any more of their precious time, he let her go, moving forward to rearrange the display, putting it in sequence of his mother's name. The bottles fit securely into their new slots.

She and Justin waited, but nothing happened.

Confusion seized her. "It isn't working."

"Damn it." His tone went tense. "I was so sure—"

A series of clicks silenced him.

The wall with the empty wine rack began to move. Like the electronic door that it was, it rolled open, giving them access to what was on the other side.

Maya took a much-needed breath. So did Justin. This was it. They stepped over the threshold and walked straight into a life-size vault filled with paintings, sculptures, statues, tapestries and ancient pottery.

A treasure to behold.

They wandered around, taking pictures of everything.

"Look over there," Justin said, pointing to boxes against the wall. "Who knows what's inside of those?"

"We certainly can't open them. Not now. We don't have a way to reseal them." She considered the pieces that were exposed. "There could be paintings hidden inside of other paintings. Between the canvases and the frames."

"That's true. But we can't tear anything apart. We'll just document what we can see."

She nodded, then noticed a Picasso that had sold to an anonymous buyer at Sotheby's last week. She'd read about it in the paper.

"I don't think this is stolen," she said, explaining why she thought it was a legitimate piece.

"Take a picture of it anyway. It could've gotten ripped off since then."

"You're right." She clicked the Picasso, then snapped a Warhol. They separated, and he went to work on the other side of the room.

Maya moved too quickly and got light-headed. She glanced at an abstract and started. "Does that look strange to you?"

"What?" He followed her line of sight. "I've never been into that type of stuff."

"I don't mean it like that. It's…" She struggled to clear her vision. "…melting."

He stopped, studied her. "Are you okay?"

"I don't know. I—" She stumbled, reaching for the edge of a sculpture for support.

Justin was at her side instantly, holding onto

her. "They drugged you. Damn it. They gave you something."

She teetered in his arms. She felt as if she were in a carnival fun house, only she wasn't having fun. The Picasso and Warhol were getting blurry, too. Everything was.

"They must have spiked your last drink at the party. Probably mine, too. Only I'm not feeling it yet."

"'Cause you're bigger than I am. Taller, heavier. More tolerance. What are we gonna do, Justin?"

"We're going to get the hell out of here." He kept his arm around her. "Let's go."

They walked about two steps, and the lights went out.

She gasped, and they both tripped, knocking something over.

She was scared, but she didn't want to say it out loud. The vault was beyond dark. Without windows, without any kind of outside light, it seemed like a dungeon. Maya couldn't even see Justin. But she could feel him. Thank God, she thought, as his arm tightened around her waist.

He kept guiding her in the direction of what she assumed was the door. But they never made it.

A noise caught their attention.

The door had just closed.

He cursed and tried to dial his cell phone, but there was no reception in the vault.

Maya shivered. They were trapped, drugged and alone, with someone waiting on the other side. "They're going to kill us."

Justin kept her under his wing. "No, they aren't. I won't let it happen. I promised to protect you, and I will."

But even as he said it, as he fought to stay strong, she could tell the medication was starting to affect him. He'd begun to sway a little on his feet. Sooner or later they'd both be passed out on the floor.

At the mercy of his family.

When Maya regained consciousness, the lights in the vault were back on, and she was strapped to a chair, wrists and ankles bound. Justin was in the same predicament. Their gazes locked, and she could tell that he'd just come awake, too.

"Are you all right?" he asked, shaking off his grogginess and focusing on her. "You're not hurt, are you?"

"I'm fine." Her head was buzzing, but she didn't have any physical injuries. "Are you okay?"

He nodded, and she considered the irony of being just a few untouchable feet away from him. The chairs they were tied to had come from the wine cellar table where they'd once shared an intimate dinner.

She glanced in the direction of the rolling door. It was open now, for all the good it did. They weren't going anywhere. Footsteps sounded and a suited shadow beamed over them.

Leo.

Justin turned his attention to the other man. "Well, look who's here. The Hulk himself."

The security chief all but smiled. "Always the smart guy. Even when he's in trouble."

"You call this trouble? A little dope in my system? Some nylon rope? A pretty girl beside me?"

"Yeah, genius, I do." Leo moved closer.

Justin narrowed his gaze. His eyes were still a little glassy. "How long have you had us trussed up like this?"

"About thirty minutes or so. I only gave you enough *dope,* as you so aptly put it, to knock you out for a short while. It'll wear off quickly. You won't be stoned like last time." He patted the holstered gun clipped to his belt. "I wanted both of you to be coherent when I killed you, to be aware of your executions." The security chief looked pointedly at Maya, then back at Justin. "Sweet lovers that you are."

Justin tensed. A visible tightening of muscle. But he didn't challenge Leo. He didn't rile their captor. "At least tell us why we're going to die."

"Because she's Sam Sullivan's daughter, and you're a pain in the ass. Nosing around, investigating us, listening in doorways. You shouldn't have done that."

Justin remained still, but Maya's knees were practically knocking.

Leo looked at her again, but he kept talking to Justin. "I didn't know who she was, not until a few weeks ago. And even then, it wasn't easy to find out. Her daddy kept a pretty good secret. Richard was surprised when I told him."

"What about Brian?" Justin asked.

"The boss?" Leo mocked. "Why would I tell him? He isn't in on this. Can you imagine? The control freak not knowing that we're dealing in stolen art? Hiding it among the rest of this stuff? That gives Richard such a rush."

Justin swallowed as if his mouth had gone dry. Maya's was parched, too.

Leo turned toward her. "Do you know why I killed Sam? I'll tell you." He punctuated his next words, mimicking a parental tone. "If you be a good girl and say please."

Bile rose in her throat. Justin snared her gaze, giving her a tight nod, and she realized that he wanted her to distract Leo, to keep him talking.

She could only assume that Justin was trying to untie the knots behind his back. Maya didn't know how to begin working on hers, not without getting caught, not without rattling her chair.

"Please," she told to Leo, her voice cracking.

He smiled, enjoying his position of power. "While

this place was being built, Sam used to come by now and then to oversee the construction." The security chief righted a fallen watercolor, the object Justin and Maya had knocked over in the dark. "But he wasn't supposed to find out that we planned on using his precious vault for stolen goods."

"But he did?" she asked, her voice still raw.

"Yeah, but he hadn't done it purposely. Not like you and Mr. IQ."

"Then how?" she prodded. "How?"

"Sam showed up unexpectedly one day. Richard and I thought we were alone and discovered that Sam was there and had overheard us talking about how we were pulling a fast one on Brian. We were just getting the operation started, lining up our contacts for later. Sam promised he wouldn't say anything, but we knew he was the righteous type. He wouldn't have stayed quiet for long. If he didn't go running to the cops, he would've told Brian."

She tempered the urge to vomit, to purge her fear. What if Justin couldn't get loose before Leo unholstered his gun?

"I strangled your dad." The killer gripped his own throat. "Like this. There was no blood. Nothing to trace."

"What did you do with his body?"

"I hauled it away with some construction material and took it to the Halloway's beach house. It was being renovated at the time, and Richard told me to put it beneath the forms for a new driveway. Clever, huh? A cement burial."

When Leo turned bone-cold silent, Maya panicked. She couldn't think of anything else to say, to keep the conversation going, to buy more time. Images of her father's body swam in her mind.

Then Justin spoke. "What are you going to do?" he asked the security chief. "Hide our bodies until you can haul us away, too? No one is going to believe that we just up and disappeared."

"No one knows that Maya is Sam's daughter. They won't make the connection. And you're not going to disappear. I'm going to leave your bodies out in the open."

"And incriminate yourself? Come on, Leo."

"Come on what? The cameras were dismantled and a blank tape is running. It'll look like part of the crime, thanks to you. The police won't be able to identify the shooter." He patted his weapon. "I'm not sporting a registered gun."

"What about the stolen art? If this becomes a crime scene—"

"We're not storing any hot goods right now. But either way, I took your cell phones. We don't want the cops to wonder why you were snapping pictures." Leo made a dramatic pause. "Brian will be devastated when you turn up dead. He'll assume that one of our old enemies infiltrated the party, followed you down here and forced you to let him into the locked cellar, seeking vengeance and murdering Denny's beloved grandson. The sexy girlfriend, too," he added, moving toward Maya.

He knelt in front of her. He was wearing gloves, keeping his fingerprints to himself. He messed with her hair, pushing it away from her face. Her skin crawled as if worms were seeping into her pores.

Time ticked by. Seconds. Minutes. Sickening silence. She couldn't look over at Justin, and he couldn't see her. The other man blocked their way.

"You're hotter than I gave you credit for." Leo rubbed a finger over her mouth, smearing her lipstick. "You and lover boy that night in the wine cellar, getting nasty with each other. I enjoyed the show."

She wanted to spit at him, to exhibit every ounce of her disgust, but she wasn't about to trigger his temper. Since his back was turned to Justin, she could only pray that—

"Get away from my woman," Justin said suddenly.

Leo laughed. "Listen to him. The noble savage." He reached for his gun and spun around to face his nemesis.

Only he didn't have time to fire.

Free from his bonds, Justin lunged, knocking the 9mm out of the security chief's hand.

Both men dived for the weapon. Paintings toppled, sculptures shook, pottery rattled. They tumbled back and forth, fighting over the gun.

Then it went off. Boom. Just like that.

Oh God…Oh God…Oh God…

Justin had been hit.

Maya could see the shocked pain on his face, the blood coloring his shirt. But he didn't stop fighting.

Her lungs constricted, and another shot rang out. This time it hit Leo. His shirt stained red, too.

Justin climbed to his knees, but Leo didn't move. Maya watched as her lover checked Leo's pulse.

"He's alive," Justin said, leaning over the unconscious man. "But the son of a bitch needs an ambulance."

Her breath remained lodged in her throat. Justin retrieved his cell phone, picked up Leo's gun and came toward her. After he untied her, they held each other as desperately as the situation would allow.

"You need an ambulance, too." The sticky warmth of his blood seeped between them. He'd been shot in the shoulder, and the bullet was probably still lodged in his body.

Maya wanted to tell him that she loved him, to admit how he deeply he affected her. But she couldn't.

She was still afraid of making a commitment, of being part of his future. He was a good man, an honorable man, but the Halloways would always be a deep, dark part of him.

Looking into his eyes, she struggled to bandage his wound, tying her sash around it, doing her best to stem the bloody flow.

They exited the vault and walked out of the phony cellar, intending to call 9-1-1 and get the authorities involved.

But before they could summon help, they ran straight into Hutch.

Chapter 13

Justin gripped the 9mm and raised it at the gallery manager.

"I'm armed, too," Hutch said. "But there's no reason to go there. I'm on your side."

"Sure you are." The pain from Justin's wound was rising, but he wasn't going to let it show.

Hutch explained his presence. "I noticed that you and Maya were missing from the party. Then I realized that Leo was gone, too."

"Leo is back there with a bullet in his stomach."

"You're injured, too."

Justin didn't budge. He wouldn't give Hutch the

satisfaction of knowing how light-headed he was. "I'll live."

The other man barely raised a brow. "What about Leo?"

"He was alive when we left him."

"Did he kill Sam Sullivan?" Hutch asked.

At the mention of her father's name, Maya tensed. If Hutch made a move toward her, Justin would fire the weapon.

"Yes. He killed Sam. He told us the location of the body, too. We know everything we need to know. But we're not sharing that information with you."

"Yes, you are. But first, put down the gun and let me call for backup."

"Backup?" Justin stared at him. "Who the hell are you?"

Hutch didn't break the stare. "Who do you think I am? Listen to me, Justin. I've known all along about Maya. I investigated her and everyone else who works for the Halloways. Why do you think I'm so familiar with Sam, too?"

"Because you're a federal agent," Justin said. "Or that's your story. That's what you're trying to get us to believe."

"It isn't a story. I couldn't tell Maya who I was, so I tried to come up with a way for her to feel comfortable around me, to trust me."

"By behaving like Sam? She did trust you. Until we found out that you were in business with Leo."

"I was hoping you'd know the difference. That you'd figure out that I was one of the good guys. The Bureau helped me land the job at the gallery. They created a background for me that Richard and Leo couldn't resist. I've been posing as an art smuggler, moving counterfeit pieces, making Richard and Leo think they're real. But I was brought in to investigate Sam's disappearance. We suspected that he was dead and that it might've had something to do with the art vault he'd built."

"But you couldn't prove it."

"No, we couldn't." He took a quick glance at Maya. "I'm sorry about your father." He turned back to Justin. "Now put down the gun."

Still protecting Maya, Justin squinted. "Call for backup first. Prove who you say you are. Who you seem to be."

Hutch did just that. He summoned more FBI. He called the paramedics, too. But Justin wasn't going to accept medical attention. Not until he saw Richard go down.

"I want to be there when you arrest my uncle."

Hutch agreed, and the party turned to chaos. Leo was taken away in an ambulance, and Richard was handcuffed, sandwiched between two feds.

Justin walked up to him. "I wanted to like you. I

wanted you to be innocent. Now I just want to see you be some other inmate's bitch."

Richard's jaw clenched. "I shouldn't have trusted Leo to kill you. I should have done it myself. Beverly's beloved son. Denny's prince. I despised you from the moment I found out you existed. If it'd been up to me, I would have driven a stake through your heart then."

"But you didn't, and now you never will. You weren't the underboss of this family. You were the underbelly."

Richard tried to jerk his handcuffs and got a harder jerk from one of the feds. Justin had struck a chord.

While the prisoner was led away, he went into a tirade, shouting that he should've been the boss. He hated Brian for disbanding the mob, and he hated their dad for not caring that Richard was robbed of moving up the ranks.

Brian stood by, his face stricken with grief. Tall and trim and struggling to keep his dignity, he barely moved, barely blinked.

After Richard was gone, he approached Justin and Maya. Silence stretched between them. The fancy ballroom, with its retreating guests, seemed like a morgue.

"Go to the hospital," Brian said, reaching out to touch Justin, but stopping before he made contact. "And I'll call your parents."

Justin didn't know what to say. He'd never been close to Brian. But he could tell that the other man was sorry. That he would do whatever he could to make up for the devastation his brother had caused.

Maya went with Justin to the emergency room, and he held her hand, hoping they could put the shattered pieces of their lives back together.

"Stay with me," he said.

"I will," she promised.

Giving in to the exhaustion, to the pain, he closed his eyes and wondered if she meant "for now" or "forever."

With Maya, he couldn't be sure.

Maya had been at the hospital all night. Justin's parents were there, too. They'd flown in from Texas and had arrived after his surgery. Justin's sister was in Europe, where she would remain. His parents didn't want to subject their daughter to her brother's mob-triggered plight.

Maya glanced at her lover. The bullet had been removed from his shoulder, and he was asleep, dozing from the medication he'd been given. He'd already been monitored in the post-anesthesia care unit and had been moved to a regular room, where he was now.

Heather, his mother, stepped closer to his bed. She watched her son through troubled eyes. Michael,

Justin's father, stood beside a window. It was morning, and the sun gleamed through the glass, brightening the dimly decorated room. Visiting hours had just begun.

"This is why we never told him that he was related to the Halloways," Heather said.

"I know. I'm sorry." Maya wanted to curl up beside Justin, to feel the warmth of his body next to hers. But she wanted to run away, too. Nothing inside her made any sense.

"They'll probably release him tomorrow," Michael said, even though he was frowning. "He's going to be all right."

Heather's voice caught. "What if he'd been killed?"

Silent, Maya studied the other woman's pale blond hair and Anglo features. She examined Michael's Native cheekbones and broad shoulders, too. Justin could have been the mixed-blood child they'd conceived.

Heather sat in a plastic chair next to her son's bed. "You both could have been killed."

"What happened to the bastard who caught the other bullet?" Michael asked Maya. "The security chief? Did he survive? Has the hospital told you anything about him?"

"Leo pulled through. He had surgery, too. As soon as he recovers, he'll be transported to a federal prison. For now they have armed guards at his door."

Heather made a tight face. "I think Justin will want to stay at the mansion. To make things right with Brian. He'll want to get to know him better."

Maya shivered. Suddenly the room seemed cold. "He already got to know his grandfather."

Michael frowned again. "This is our worst nightmare. Justin bonding with Denny Halloway."

"Justin should hate Denny for putting a hit on Reed," Heather added. "But he blames Reed instead. My brother would be heartbroken if he knew that the Halloways had kidnapped his adult son and made him one of their own."

Maya didn't know how to respond. Heather and Michael's world had been turned upside down, and she was part of it. Justin hadn't reported the kidnapping because he'd promised to help her. She'd pulled him deeper into the Halloway mess.

"Do you love him?" Heather asked suddenly.

Dear God. She wanted to lie, to pretend that her feelings hadn't gone that far, but she couldn't. "Yes."

"Does he love you, too?"

"I think so." She reached for the necklace he'd given her. She'd been wearing it almost every day, but she hadn't put a lock of his hair inside it. The Cherokee rose was empty. "He asked me to stay with him."

"Are you going to?"

"I—" Maya stalled, still etching the ivory flower, still feeling its jeweled surface. "I don't want to be connected to the Halloways, not any more than I already am. But I don't want to lose your son. I don't want to let him go."

"But you might," Heather said, her voice soft, sad.

"Yes," Maya admitted.

She might leave the man she loved.

Maya spent three days at the mansion with Justin, giving him time to heal. His shoulder was bandaged and his arm was in a sling, but he was on the mend. He seemed to have a high tolerance for pain.

Physical pain, she thought. Emotionally, he seemed spent. He watched her pack her bags, and she prayed that she was doing the right thing. That life would be easier for both of them once she was gone.

Justin's mother was right. He'd decided to stay at the mansion. He wanted to get to know Brian, to give his "innocent" uncle a chance. But he intended to commute back and forth to Texas, too. He was trying to hold on to both sides of his family.

As for Maya, her family was truly gone. She'd known all along that her father was dead, but that didn't lessen her grief. The FBI had recovered his body, and his wife and sons would be giving him a proper burial. Maya wouldn't be there. She'd asked Hutch not to reveal her identity to Sam's loved ones. They didn't need to hear about the affair he'd had with her mother, not now, not while the news that he'd been murdered was so fresh. Later, she would talk to them. She didn't have a choice. The truth wouldn't be repressed at the trial.

A knock sounded on the door, and she abandoned her suitcase to answer it. Justin came with her.

Brian stood on the other side. "May I come in?"

She nodded and stepped back.

He entered the suite, made eye contact with his nephew, then turned toward her.

"I'm sorry about your dad," he said. "Sam was a good man. I liked him."

"Thank you." She kept her emotions close to the vest, refusing to break down in front of him.

"I had no idea he was your father," he added. "Not until after Richard was arrested."

She remained silent, and he spoke to her again. "When Richard told Justin about the wine cellar, he was also supposed to explain that it was an art vault. He was supposed to tell Justin that the bottles were coded."

"Did you ask Richard why he didn't?"

"Yes, and he said that he wanted to wait until he found a Frida Kahlo original for you. We'd already given Justin a Remington, so he thought we should give you an art gift. That we should store it in the vault, then take you and Justin there to see it, to surprise you." The former mobster shook his head. "I believed him. I believed everything my brother said."

Maya didn't comment.

Brian went on, finishing his story. "Building the vault was Richard's idea to begin with. When he heard about the one your dad had designed for Kane Carter, he came to me and asked if we could hire Sam to design one for our expanding art collection. A false wine cellar that opened into a vault. I loved the idea, too." He hesitated for a moment. "In fact, it got me thinking about Beverly's interest in rare wine. I asked Sam if we could have the bottles custom made instead of using the generic vintages that were normally provided, and he referred me to the company that manufactures the bottles. But Dad was right. The cellar is tainted. I should tear it down."

Maya's voice vibrated. "None of this is your fault."

Brian cleared his throat. "I wish you weren't leaving. I wish you'd reconsider."

She changed the subject. "Just promise me one thing. That you'll treat Tori well. That you won't keep hurting her."

Brian stiffened. "I don't hurt Tori."

"You cheat on her."

He made a face. "I don't." His expression turned even tighter. "I used to, but that was in the beginning before she grew on me so damn much."

"Then tell her," Maya said. "Be honest."

"I'd rather not get that close."

"You'd rather let her think you're still seeing other women?"

"She's young and beautiful. She'll find someone else someday."

"Maybe. But she'll probably always love you."

"Love is a tricky thing." He divided his gaze between her and Justin. "But I'm sure you two know that better than anyone."

He created an awkward moment, then apologized for taking up so much of their time and turned and left, closing the door behind him.

"He's right," Justin said. "We do know."

Her heart lodged in her throat. She'd been dreading this conversation.

He moved closer. "I love you, Maya. I'd been thinking about it, worrying about it, but I finally accepted it on the night of your party. The night everything went down."

"It happened to me, too," she admitted. "But it was before then."

"Then give us a chance. Don't go." He reached for her, circling her with his good arm. "Marry me."

Her pulse pounded so hard, she could barely hear herself think. He'd just proposed. He'd just asked her to make a lifelong commitment. "What's different this time, Justin? You were engaged once before."

"You're different. The way you make me feel. You could buy a wedding dress tomorrow and I'd whisk you down the aisle as soon as you'd let me." He brought her closer to his heart. "When I told you that I'd die for you, I meant it. I love you the way a man should love a woman."

She didn't say anything. She couldn't. Her pulse was still pounding.

He proposed again. "Be my wife. Be part of me. Part of my family."

Oh, God. "Being part of your family is what scares me."

He didn't give up. "Stay here one more night. Don't run when the chips are down. Face your fears."

"One night," she agreed, immersed in the familiarity of his touch, in the love-swept danger that clung to him. "One last night."

At bedtime, Justin didn't turn off the light. He left an amber lamp burning, and it washed the room in a warm hue. Maya lay next to him, and they were both silent. Lester slept in his doggie bed on the floor. The puppy was snoring.

Finally Maya spoke. "Do you think they dream?"

"Who? Dogs? I don't know. But Lester seems happy all the time."

"Yes, he does. I guess it's not as easy for people to be that happy. That content. We always seem to have obstacles in our way."

He turned toward her. She looked angelic in the soft light. Her hair was loose, and her nightgown was white and lacy. He couldn't imagine living without

Maya. He could only hope and pray that she changed her mind. That she would give their future a chance.

"I haven't been totally honest," he said, recalling the advice she'd given Brian. "I asked you to face your fears. But I haven't faced mine."

She met his gaze. "About me? Are you having second thoughts?"

"No, never. I'm sure about how much I love you. You'll never have to worry about that. My fear is about Reed. I have the power to bring him home."

Maya blinked at him. "I don't understand."

He took a deep breath and explained, telling her what Denny had told him.

"Oh my goodness, Justin. Oh, my God. Do your parents know?"

"No. You're the first person I've confided in. But it's time for me to try to accept Reed. To give him the benefit of the doubt." He reached out to touch a strand of her hair. "I want to bring everyone together the best I can. You, my parents, my sister, Brian. But I can't do that, not if I leave Reed out. He's part of me, too."

"Maybe Denny is lying. Maybe he'll have Reed killed the minute he comes home."

"He wouldn't do that. Not to Beverly, and not to me. Denny loved his daughter, and I think in his own strange way, he loves me, too."

Her eyes locked onto his. "So do I. Only my love isn't strange."

"No, it's fearful, and I think maybe that's worse. It shouldn't matter if I'm an Elk or a Halloway."

"I wish you'd forget about them."

"I can't. If I do, I'll be running from my roots, from a stigma I'll never be able to escape. If I embrace it, if I accept it, I won't have to live in shame. And neither will my children." He didn't let go of her hair. He kept it softly twined between his fingers. "Kids I want to have with you."

She managed a shaky smile. "Sam would have liked you. He wanted me to have a family someday." Her smile fell. "But I'm not ready for this."

"Because of what Richard did? Don't punish me for his sins."

Her voice shook. "I'm not. Not in the way you mean."

He frowned. "Are sure you don't want to go to Sam's funeral? I can go with you. We can slip into the back of the church."

She shook her head. "I'll bury him in my own way."

"So you can keep his secret a while longer?" Justin sighed. "The secrets in my family aren't protecting anyone any more. As soon as I tell my parents about Reed, everything will be out in the open."

"Your parents are going back to Texas tomorrow."

"I'm going to tell them first thing in the morning. And I'm going to tell them that I asked you to marry me, too. But I'll give you as much time as you need to reconsider. I'll wait as long as I have to."

She closed her eyes, and he knew she was going to cry.

He held her while her tears fell. She was grieving, he thought, purging her pain, missing her father and fighting what she felt for Justin.

And all he could do was be there for her.

The following day, Justin left to talk to his parents, who were at a nearby hotel, and Maya wandered into her studio to pack her supplies, still battling her emotions.

She understood why Heather and Michael had decided not to stay at the Halloways' while they were in town. They didn't want to be affiliated with the Mob Mansion.

And neither did Maya.

She glanced at the half-finished painting of the little angel and thought about Justin's grandfather. He'd figured out that the babies had been switched. He'd helped uncover Justin's identity.

She looked at an empty canvas she'd set aside for her next project: a *calaca* of Beverly. She wondered how Denny would feel about her painting a joyful skeleton of his daughter.

Confused, Maya closed her eyes. Her art career had changed. She could make a living at it now. She'd earned a substantial income from the gallery show. But she'd just as soon give it to charity, to get rid of everything the Halloways had provided, everything connected to them.

Even Justin? The man she loved?

God help her, she thought. God help them both. Last night she'd cried herself to sleep in his arms. And this morning she'd awakened to him brushing his lips across her forehead and leaving her alone.

Needing a diversion, she left her studio and went into the den, where the Halloways displayed their family photos. If she married Justin, if she had his children, their pictures would be on these walls.

She spent about twenty minutes gazing at each and every image, then she turned and discovered that Tori had walked into the room.

"I've been looking for you," the blonde said.

"You have?"

Tori nodded. "To say goodbye. Are you really leaving?"

"I don't know. I'm fighting it." She noticed that the other woman was dressed in her usual sexy attire. Maya wore a pair of jeans and a simple shirt. Her mistress days were over. "Did Brian talk to you?"

"About what?"

"Nothing. Never mind." She dropped the subject. Apparently Brian hadn't told Tori that he was being faithful. But Brian was afraid of love. It was the reason he was so guarded, so distant.

Like Maya.

She winced, realizing how much she had in common with Justin's uncle.

"I can't believe what Richard and Leo did," Tori said. "And that you and Justin caught them. You're like one of the Hardy boys and Nancy Drew."

Maya couldn't help but smile. "I think we're more like Steed and Mrs. Peel."

The blonde scrunched her nose. "Who?"

"Old TV spies. Cult-classic types."

"I heard that the Hardy Boys and Nancy Drew used to be on TV, too. But I read the books when I was a kid. They were my escape."

From a troubled childhood, Maya thought. No matter how soiled Tori's life had been, she'd tried to keep her heart pure.

"You're a nice girl," Maya said.

"Thanks." The other woman grinned. Her breasts were spilling out of a too-tight top. "I don't think anyone has ever said that to me." She turned serious. "I hope you stay with Justin. You seem good together."

"He's everything to me. If I leave, I'm going to miss him so much. I already feel empty inside, and I'm not even gone yet."

"Then leaving doesn't make much sense, does it?"

"No, it doesn't." And neither did being afraid, not facing her fears.

Maya ended her talk with Tori and went back to her suite to wait for Justin.

Her best friend. Her lover. The man who'd admitted that he would die for her. How could she live without him? How could she let his Halloway bloodlines stand in their way?

She couldn't. Not without leaving a gaping hole in her heart. In his. In a future that was meant to be.

When he arrived, she wanted to rush toward him. But Lester beat her to the punch. So she stood back, meeting Justin's gaze from across the living room.

"My mom cried," he said, after he greeted the puppy. "She bawled like a baby when I told her that Reed could come home. I think my dad cried, too. His eyes got kind of watery."

Unable to hold back, she blurted what was on her mind. "I want to marry you, Justin. I want to be part of you, of your family. I want to wake up every day beside you. I want to have your children. Elk, Halloway or Blackwood," she added, thinking about Reed. "It doesn't matter what your last name is. As long as you're my husband."

He walked toward her, and she could see the relief on his face, the wonder, the he-couldn't-wait-to-claim-her joy.

"We'll make it work. We'll make our lives feel normal." He reached for her. "As normal as we can."

"For a man who was born into the mob and a woman who paints skeletons for a living?"

He swept her into a one-armed hug, pressing her tight against his body. "We do sound a little odd."

"Because we are."

He smiled, and she kissed him, soft and slow and filled with hope. She was *never, ever* letting him go again.

Epilogue

The aroma of a home-cooked meal wafted through the air. Pot roast and mashed potatoes, Justin thought. Green beans seasoned with bits of bacon. Blueberry pie and fresh whipping cream.

Food for a family gathering.

Justin and Maya were at his parents' red-and-white farmhouse, waiting for Reed and his wife to arrive.

This was it. The day of reckoning.

He took Maya's hand and led her onto the porch. The Texas Hill Country air was warm, and in the distance, limestone caves provided a cavernous backdrop. Lester followed them, curling up below the swing, much like Justin's original dog used to do.

"I love this place," Maya said. "I love knowing that you grew up here."

Justin took a deep breath. Memories were everywhere, in the trees, in the grass, in the scent of hay and horses.

"I love it, too. But I wonder if I was restless most of my life because I sensed that something was wrong."

"That you weren't who you seemed to be?"

He nodded, and she leaned against the porch rail. Her hair fell long and loose, blowing softly in the breeze. They weren't married yet. They'd decided to wait to set a date, to give everyone a chance to be there, including Reed and his wife.

"Are you nervous, Justin?"

"I'm trying not to be." But he knew he still had a long road ahead of him. "This is an ambitious undertaking."

"Meeting your biological father? Planning a wedding with the Halloways?"

"Yeah. But at least my parents have accepted them. And my sister will be home from Europe soon. She'll get to know them, too." In addition to Brian and Tori, who'd finally learned that her former-mobster lover had quit cheating, Justin had cousins, nieces and nephews who'd always be part of the mix.

"Did you talk to your grandfather today?" Maya asked.

"He called this morning." Justin pictured Denny, standing in the prison yard with a pay phone pressed to his ear. "He isn't thrilled about me getting to know Reed, but he thinks Beverly would be pleased. That she'll be looking down on us."

"I think so, too."

Just then a white Dually turned onto the road leading to the farmhouse. Lester perked up, and Justin's pulse went into triple time. "They're here."

The vehicle moved closer, and a man and woman came into view. Justin tried to see his father clearly through the windshield, but the late-day sun glared upon the glass.

Finally Reed parked and got out of the truck. He was tall and trim, athletic for a man in his fifties. He reached behind the seat and lifted a cowboy hat, seating it firmly on his head, adjusting the brim so it didn't shield his eyes. He went around to the other side and opened the door for his wife. She was small and blond.

Reed and his wife walked forward, and Justin and Maya met them halfway. The foursome stood in the graveled driveway and gazed at each other. The dog watched from the porch.

Finally Maya broke the ice. She introduced herself to Reed's wife, whose name was Emily.

The men still hadn't spoken.

Reed looked as if he could barely breathe. "I'm sorry," he said to Justin. "I thought I was doing the right thing. Protecting you from the mob. Giving you a good, safe life without me. I should have kept in touch, but if I talked to you over the phone, if I wrote you letters, it would've made missing you that much worse. It was the only way I knew how to cope with letting you go."

Justin's throat clogged. "It's okay. I understand. I didn't at first, but I do now."

"There wasn't a day that went by that I didn't think about you. My baby boy. My son." Reed's voice went rough. He turned in the direction of the hills. "The last time I saw you was in one of the caves. Michael and Heather brought you to me while I was running from the mob and negotiating with the feds. We picked that location because Michael and I used to hang out there when we were teenagers. It was our secret place." He turned back to Justin. "You were ten months old. I wrapped you in my arms and you put your head on my shoulder. Heather cried that day, and Michael promised that he would raise my son. That he would love him like his own."

"And he has. He's been an amazing dad." A pause. A nervous question. "Do you have any other kids?"

"No. Emily and I talked about it. But in the end, I couldn't do it. I couldn't father another child knowing that I'd left one behind." Reed smiled a little. "I helped raise Emily's younger brother, though. He's married now and has two little girls. Next time you can meet him and his family."

"That'd be nice." Justin shifted his feet. "So what's your new name? Who have you been all these years?"

"James Dalton. I've been living in a small town in Idaho, where I met Emily." He glanced at his wife. "When I first met her, she reminded me of Beverly. I missed your mom so much. But later I realized that Emily wasn't Beverly, and that I couldn't go back in time. I fell in love with Emily for who she is, not for who I wanted her to be."

"I'm glad you found someone," Justin told the man who'd given him up. "I'm glad you haven't been alone."

"Thank you. That means the world to me."

Reed stepped forward, and they embraced, father to long-lost son. Being this close to Reed felt oddly familiar, and Justin wondered if he was reliving babyhood memories. Either way, it felt right. They seemed like mirror images of each other. Not physically, but emotionally. Inside, they were the same.

They separated, and the door to the farmhouse opened. Justin's mother came outside and squealed. She dashed down the porch steps and flung herself into her brother's arms. He picked her up and swung her around, making her skirt swish around her ankles.

Justin glanced at Maya and smiled. Reed's wife was smiling, too.

Michael joined the reunion. He and Reed grinned

like the rebellious teenagers they used to be, then joked about how old they were now. When they bent their heads and spoke quietly, Justin sensed that Reed was thanking Michael for being such a good father to his son.

Later, everyone joined hands at the dinner table, saying grace, repeating a Cherokee prayer Justin had learned when he was a child.

After the meal, he and Maya returned to the porch to watch the sun go down. He leaned over to kiss her, and she skimmed his cheek.

"Should we get married here or at the mansion?" she asked.

"I don't know. It's cozy here, but I met you at the mansion. That seems fitting, too."

"We'll figure it out." She smiled. "Did you know that your name means just, righteous?"

"Imagine that? Justin means just." He teased her, but he understood what she was trying to convey. With all of the family forgiveness going on, his name made sense.

But he couldn't have explored his identity without her. He couldn't have put his demons to rest. Having her by his side made him stronger, more determined.

For Justin, there was no one like Maya.

No one at all.

* * * * *

THE ROYAL HOUSE OF NIROLI
Always passionate, always proud

The richest royal family in the world—united by
blood and passion,
torn apart by deceit and desire.

Nestled in the azure blue of the Mediterranean Sea,
the majestic island of Niroli has prospered for cen-
turies. The Fierezza men have worn the crown with
passion and pride since ancient times. But now, as the
king's health declines, and his two sons have been
tragically killed, the crown is in jeopardy.

The clock is ticking—a new heir must be found
before the king is forced to abdicate. By royal decree
the internationally scattered members of the Fierezza
family are summoned to claim their destiny. But any
person who takes the throne must do so according to
The Rules of the Royal House of Niroli. Soon secrets
and rivalries emerge as the descendents of this
ancient royal line vie for position and power. Only a
true Fierezza can become ruler—a person dedicated
to their country, their people…and their eternal love!

Each month starting in July 2007,
Harlequin Presents is delighted to bring you
an exciting installment from
THE ROYAL HOUSE OF NIROLI,
in which you can follow the epic search
for the true Nirolian king.
Eight heirs, eight romances, eight fantastic stories!

Here's your chance to enjoy a sneak preview of
the first book delivered to you by royal decree....

FIVE MINUTES later she was standing immobile in front of the study's window, her original purpose of coming in forgotten, as she stared in shocked horror at the envelope she was holding. Waves of heat followed by icy chills surged through her body. She could hardly see the address now through her blurred vision, but the crest on its left-hand front corner stood out, its *royal* crest, followed by the address: *HRH Prince Marco of Niroli...*

She didn't hear Marco's key in the apartment door, she didn't even hear him calling out her name. Her shock was so great that nothing could penetrate

it. It encased her in a kind of bubble, which only con-
centrated the torment of what she was suffering and
branded it on her brain so that it could never be forgotten. It was only finally pierced by the sudden
opening of the study door as Marco walked in.

"Welcome home, *Your Highness*. I suppose I ought
to curtsy." She waited, praying that he would laugh and
tell her that she had got it all wrong, that the envelope
she was holding, addressing him as Prince Marco of
Niroli, was some silly mistake. But like a tiny candle
flame shivering vulnerably in the dark, her hope trem-
bled fearfully. And then the look in Marco's eyes ex-
tinguished it as cruelly as a hand placed callously over
a dying person's face to stem their last breath.

"Give that to me," he demanded, taking the envelope from her.

"It's too late, Marco," Emily told him brokenly. "I
know the truth now…." She dug her teeth in her
lower lip to try to force back her own pain.

"You had no right to go through my desk," Marco
shot back at her furiously, full of loathing at being
caught off-guard and forced into a position in which
he was in the wrong, making him determined to find
something he could accuse Emily of. "I trusted you…."

Emily could hardly believe what she was hearing.
"No, you didn't trust me, Marco, and you didn't trust
me because you knew that I couldn't trust you. And
you knew that because you're a liar, and liars don't

trust people because they know that they themselves cannot be trusted." She not only felt sick, she also felt as though she could hardly breathe. "You are Prince Marco of Niroli…. How could you not tell me who you are and still live with me as intimately as we have lived together?" she demanded brokenly.

"Stop being so ridiculously dramatic," Marco demanded fiercely. "You are making too much of the situation."

"*Too much?*" Emily almost screamed the words at him. "When were you going to tell me, Marco? Perhaps you just planned to walk away without telling me anything? After all, what do my feelings matter to you?"

"Of course they matter." Marco stopped her sharply. "And it was in part to protect them, and you, that I decided not to inform you when my grandfather first announced that he intended to step down from the throne and hand it on to me."

"To protect me?" Emily nearly choked on her fury. "Hand on the throne? No wonder you told me when you first took me to bed that all you wanted was sex. You *knew* that was the only kind of relationship there could ever be between us! You *knew* that one day you would be Niroli's king. No doubt you are expected to marry a princess. Is she picked out for you already, your *royal* bride?"

* * * * *

*Look for THE FUTURE KING'S PREGNANT
MISTRESS
by Penny Jordan in July 2007,
from Harlequin Presents,
available wherever books are sold.*

HARLEQUIN®

Mediterranean NIGHTS™

Experience the glamour and elegance of cruising the high seas with a new 12-book series....

MEDITERRANEAN NIGHTS

Coming in July 2007...

SCENT OF A WOMAN

by

Joanne Rock

When Danielle Chevalier is invited to an exclusive conference aboard *Alexandra's Dream,* she knows it will mean good things for her struggling fragrance company. But her dreams get a setback when she meets Adam Burns, a representative from a large American conglomerate.

Danielle is charmed by the brusque American— until she finds out he means to compete with her bid for the opportunity that will save her family business!

nocturne™

**DON'T MISS THE RIVETING CONCLUSION
TO THE RAINTREE TRILOGY**

RAINTREE: SANCTUARY

by *New York Times* bestselling author

BEVERLY
BARTON

Mercy, guardian of the Raintree
homeplace, takes a stand against
the Ansara wizards to battle for
the Clan's future.

*On sale July,
wherever books are sold.*

SNRT2

Silhouette®

Desire

THE GARRISONS

A brand-new family saga begins with

THE CEO'S SCANDALOUS AFFAIR

BY ROXANNE ST. CLAIRE

Eldest son Parker Garrison is preoccupied running
his Miami hotel empire and dealing with his recently
deceased father's secret second family. Since he has
little time to date, taking his superefficient assistant
to a charity event should have been a simple plan.
Until passion takes them beyond business.

Don't miss any of the six exciting titles in
THE GARRISONS continuity, beginning in July.
Only from Silhouette Desire.

THE CEO'S SCANDALOUS AFFAIR

#1807

Available July 2007.

REQUEST YOUR
FREE BOOKS!

2 FREE NOVELS PLUS 2 FREE GIFTS!

Silhouette® Romantic

SUSPENSE

Sparked by Danger, Fueled by Passion!

YES! Please send me 2 FREE Silhouette® Romantic Suspense novels and my 2 FREE gifts. After receiving them, if I don't wish to receive any more books, I can return the shipping statement marked "cancel." If I don't cancel, I will receive 4 brand-new novels every month and be billed just $4.24 per book in the U.S., or $4.99 per book in Canada, plus 25¢ shipping and handling per book plus applicable taxes, if any*. That's a savings of at least 15% off the cover price! I understand that accepting the 2 free books and gifts places me under no obligation to buy anything. I can always return a shipment and cancel at any time. Even if I never buy another book from Silhouette, the two free books and gifts are mine to keep forever.

240 SDN EEX6   340 SDN EEYJ

Name	(PLEASE PRINT)	
Address		Apt. #
City	State/Prov.	Zip/Postal Code

Signature (if under 18, a parent or guardian must sign)

Mail to the **Silhouette Reader Service™**:

IN U.S.A.: P.O. Box 1867, Buffalo, NY 14240-1867
IN CANADA: P.O. Box 609, Fort Erie, Ontario L2A 5X3

Not valid to current Silhouette Intimate Moments subscribers.

Want to try two free books from another line?
Call 1-800-873-8635 or visit www.morefreebooks.com.

* Terms and prices subject to change without notice. NY residents add applicable sales tax. Canadian residents will be charged applicable provincial taxes and GST. This offer is limited to one order per household. All orders subject to approval. Credit or debit balances in a customer's account(s) may be offset by any other outstanding balance owed by or to the customer. Please allow 4 to 6 weeks for delivery.

Your Privacy: Silhouette is committed to protecting your privacy. Our Privacy Policy is available online at www.eHarlequin.com or upon request from the Reader Service. From time to time we make our lists of customers available to reputable firms who may have a product or service of interest to you. If you would prefer we not share your name and address, please check here. ☐

SRS07

Romantic

SUSPENSE

COMING NEXT MONTH

#1471 ONE STORMY NIGHT—Marilyn Pappano
Jennifer Randall poses as her twin to bring down her brother-in-law whom she believes brutally attacked her sister. Little does she know that the next-door neighbor she's falling for is investigating the same man.

#1472 MY SPY—Marie Ferrarella
Mission: Impassioned
When the prime minister of England discovers his daughter has been kidnapped, he turns to the one man who can return her safely. Joshua Lazlo has rescued plenty of damsels in distress, but none has compared to his latest assignment. She's more than a handful for him and the kidnappers, but there's something about his feisty target he can't resist.

#1473 FORTUNE HUNTER'S HERO—Linda Turner
Broken Arrow Ranch
He must stay at his newly inherited ranch or ownership reverts to a secret heir. She claims a Spanish mine is located on the property. Together they set out to solve the puzzle and fight an attraction that threatens more than their hearts.

#1474 SECRETS RISING—Suzanne McMinn
Haven
In the wake of a personal tragedy, Detective Jake Mallory comes to the small town of Haven to find some peace and quiet. Instead, he finds himself caught up in a series of bizarre events that all circle around a beautiful woman. But the more he investigates, the more questions arise. And the biggest question has yet to be answered…what, or who, is buried in Keely Schiffer's backyard?

SRSCNM0607